Tales from the Subatomic Zoo

To Jane

It has been great meeting and working with you. I hope you enjoy the book!

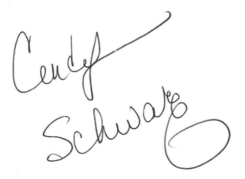

Cindy Schwarz

Tales from the Subatomic Zoo

Stories and poems about subatomic particles
written by students at Vassar College
Edited and Compiled by Cindy Schwarz

Four stories are loose adaptations of the following:
Snow White and the Seven Dwarfs – Grimm Brothers
Jack and the Beanstalk – Grimm Brothers
Jurassic Park – Michael Crichton
Alice's Adventures in Wonderland – Lewis Carroll

Glossary adapted from the glossary in *A Tour of the Subatomic Zoo: A Guide to Particle Physics* with permission from Springer-Verlag.

First printing 2002

ISBN 0-9722623-0-X

Original artwork on cover by Bryan Rachmilowitz (age 10)

For Bryan and Michael

Preface

This book is the product of many years of teaching a course at Vassar College on subatomic physics. The course was created specifically for students majoring in disciplines outside of the sciences and certainly outside of physics. At Vassar there is no requirement for taking a science course prior to graduation and the course grew out of my concern about science literacy. The course has been taught almost every year since 1987 with a total enrollment of over 400 students. The course is an overview of the field of particle physics, including the historical views of matter since the beginning of the 20th century. The course focuses not only on the facts but also on the process of learning about what the world is made of, including the interdependence of theory and experiment. As a final exercise in the course, the students were required to write a short story or poem with subatomic particles as the main characters. When I first assigned this project, I assumed that I would get many stories about Ernie the electron who was always so negative and Patty the proton who fell in love with him anyway. Well, I seriously underestimated the creativity and talent of Vassar students (mind I had only been teaching here for two years). The stories and poems that they wrote over the years have continued to amaze, entertain and surprise me. I have read theses stories at physics teachers meetings and shared them with my physics colleagues and friends for many years now. I finally had the time to collect the very best of them and publish them in this book. I hope that you enjoy them as much as I have and if physics is not your expertise that you learn as much as the students who wrote them.

The works are organized in three main categories. The first set of stories can certainly be enjoyed by anyone but the topics are probably not the most relevant for children. The second group of stories is primarily based on fairytales and could be appreciated by young children. The last section consists of poems. One young woman wrote a very imaginative paper this past spring consisting of newspaper ads and it is included at the end.

By the time you finish the book, you should be familiar with common particle world events like annihilation, pair production and decay, but a glossary of terms and suggestions for further reading are included just in case.

Cindy Schwarz-Rachmilowitz
Staatsburg, NY
July 2002

Acknowledgments

First and foremost this book would not exist were it not for the Vassar students who wrote these stories and poems. I thank all of you for being students in my class and for writing a wonderful collection of stories that continues to impress and entertain me. The majority of you have been away from Vassar for many years and have gone on to be quite successful. I am so pleased that you remember the class and thank you deeply for allowing me to include your writings in this book. You are the kind of students that makes teaching worthwhile.

I also thank Vassar for being the kind of school that it is. By allowing me to develop this course and teach it over the past fifteen years, you have allowed me to grow as a teacher and contribute to the education of our students in a very unique way. In particular, I thank my colleagues in the physics department and the current Acting Dean of the Faculty, Barbara Page, for their support on this project.

My life is about teaching, but teaching is not my whole life. I must thank my family and friends for their support not only now but over the years. Dawn, getting to know you and having you as a friend has been one of the biggest assets in my life over the past year and a half. Thanks for letting me "run all this stuff" by you and for always listening. Norman, my husband, my life, I could not have done this (or much else) without your unending support and confidence in me.

Enough of the mushy stuff and back to the facts. Additionally I thank Cornell Dawson for carefully reading an early version of the manuscript and providing valuable editing advice. Thanks also to Paul Hickman, Melissa Franklin, Cathy Ezrailson and Tom O'Kuma for their comments.

Cindy

Table of Contents

Stories

Stories

OPRAH WINFREY SHOW TRANSCRIPT: "PARTICLE
DECAY IN THE '80'S, ONE PROTON'S STORY"
BY JULIA EINSPRUCH LEWIS (1989)
AMERICAN CULTURE MAJOR

(Applause...)

Oprah: Hello. Welcome to the show. (Applause) The late
T.S. Eliot once said, "Man cannot bear too much reality."
Today, in the 1980's, we face a number of realities, realities I
have tried to address on this program. (Applause) Death in
the family, the decline of morality, and today, the decay of
subatomic particles, a topic we often forget because we can't
see it happening, but a phenomenon all of us should know
more about. I welcome today's guest, a proton, who will be
speaking to us via satellite from the Fermi Lab, just outside
the Chicago area. (Applause) Hello, Ms. Proton and thank
you for agreeing to tell us your story. This is, as far as I
know, the first talk-show interview with a subatomic particle
in the history of broadcasting. (Applause)

Ms. Proton: Thanks for inviting me to the show. My story is
a simple one, but not an insignificant one.

O: Well, let's hear it. You are now a proton, but I understand
that you were once a neutron. That sounds a little confusing
to me. I want to know, and I'm sure the studio audience
shares my curiosity, how that happened... What was the
process like? Tell us everything.

P: Until recently I was, as you said, a neutron, one of 8
neutrons and 6 protons inside the nucleus of a carbon atom.

O: And what was that like?

P: It was awful. Carbon 14 is an isotope. It was a very
unstable situation. All of us wanted to form a lighter, more
stable nucleus. I wanted out. I had always felt different, like I
didn't belong.

O: Oh, I know how that feels, honey. So, how did you react to that situation?

P: Well, in a fraction of a second I decided to convert.

O: Spontaneously? Just like that? Without any outside influences or external forces?

P: That's right. It was beta decay.

O: But where did you get the energy? I hardly have enough energy to get out of bed in the morning. I mean it must have taken a lot of energy to convert from one species to another!

P: Believe it or not, it was easy. It was radioactive decay. There was no outside supply of energy. It all came from within the nucleus. It was perfectly natural.

(Applause)

O: I'm glad to hear that the studio audience is still with us. Let's get a little audience participation going. I'll take a question from the audience. Yes, you, wearing the glittering gold bustier.

Woman wearing gold lame bustier: How did you feel after your sudden transmutation? Were there any problems of adjustment?

P: No, I feel great these days. In the process I released an electron, which is, of course, negatively charged; therefore, the emission meant that I got rid of negative energy, so I feel much more positive these days.

W: I know what you mean. That's exactly how I felt when I moved to California and found EST.

P: I also released a neutrino, which didn't make that much of a difference, since this particle carries no electrical charge and has no detectable mass. But, like the electron, it also carried off some energy.

O: So, you lost an electron and a neutrino. Did you lose weight? I mean mass.

P: No, as a proton I have the same mass that I formerly had as a neutron. There is, perhaps a 1% difference. I really haven't changed except for the fact that I am now positively charged.

O: And now you occupy the nucleus of a nitrogen atom. Living happily.

P: And stably... Oh, I can't begin to tell you how nice it is to occupy a balanced nucleus.

O: I'm sure it's wonderful... and it's been wonderful having you on the show. But before you leave us, just one more question: any changes in the near future?

P: No. I like my current situation. There are 7 of us protons and 7 neutrons in the nitrogen nucleus. I now have the stability that I have always dreamed of. It would take a cyclotron to change me now.

(Applause)

O: You're an inspiration to us all, Ms. Proton, and thanks for sharing your story with us today. Tell everyone at the lab hello for me.

P: I will and thank you! (Applause)

Stories

6

SUBATOMIC SCHOOL
BY J. C. MAZZA (1990)
HISTORY MAJOR

The opening was listed in the classifieds of the Subatomic Times:

"Instructor needed for junior high school class of particles. The curriculum emphasizes teaching proper particle etiquette and behavior in the areas of spin decay, et cetera. Send resume to Principal Proton, Standard Model Middle School, Batavia, Illinois."

Jonathan Electron read these words with interest. He had felt for some time that what he needed in his life was a change of careers. Oh, he had enjoyed his days as a gravity teacher at Mediator High, but the position no longer challenged him. Once the gravitons got the knack of attracting masses towards each other, while cleverly avoiding detection, there was really little else to teach them. The thought of educating a wider variety of particles appealed to him. He sent a resume to Principal Proton. Within two weeks he had received the news he'd been hoping to hear. He had been accepted for the position, and could start in a week!

On his first day of work in his new position, Jonathan Electron took the Metropolitan Transit Authority's accelerator to the Standard Model Middle School and entered the classroom in good spirits. His good mood did not last for long, however. The students were making an awful racket and the room was in chaos. What a change, he thought, from my former students, those well behaved gravitons! In one corner sat a rowdy looking neutron casting dirty looks at a preppy kaon plus across the room. The neutron threw a proton, an electron and an antineutrino at him and vanished from sight. But the kaon laughed and tauntingly yelled, "I only live for ten to the minus ten seconds." Then he vanished before Jonathan Electron's amazed eyes. All around him he saw particles suddenly appear and disappear. In the very middle of the class a proton had picked an unfair fight with a much smaller muon antineutrino. They hit each other with so much force that they disappeared and a positive muon and a neutron flew from the explosion to take seats in the room. Then the muon disappeared!

Order had to be restored, Jonathan realized, if he were to teach them anything. So he yelled in a loud voice, "All of you find a seat and be quiet this very moment!"

Surprised and frightened, the young particles scrambled to their desks and sat staring at their new pedagogue. But no matter how hard they tried, they could not behave. Jonathan Electron didn't mind their spinning. However, the pions, kaons, lambdas and sigmas continued to vanish and throw pions, muons and even neutrons at their classmates. And there was just no stopping the particles and antiparticles from fighting and then filling the room with even more students. Jonathan was beginning to wonder what he had gotten himself into by taking this new position. Perhaps a new seating arrangement would help him to keep order.

"All right, class," he said. "I'm Mr. Electron and I'm here to teach all of you how to behave like subatomic particles. I can't teach you unless you are good. That's why I am giving you assigned seats."

"Assigned seats?" the class lamented in unison.

"That's right. I want the mesons on this side... form a hexagon. You all know your strangeness and your charge, right? Good. You learned that in grade school. Line up according to your properties." The kaons and the pions obeyed the best that they could, but they couldn't resist the temptation to decay. "Now," Jonathan Electron continued, "the baryons on this side. Another hexagon. Seating by strangeness and charge." The protons and neutrons were the least intractable, but the lambdas, sigmas and cascades insisted upon transforming themselves into other particles.

" Sit still!" Jonathan cried, to no avail.

"What about us?" the electrons, positrons, neutrinos, taus and muons started to ask. "Where do we sit?"

Jonathan was stumped. "Let's see...how can I arrange you leptons? You don't have any strangeness. The neutrinos don't even have any charge. Just sit in order of increasing mass. Neutrinos first. Taus last. Most of you are stable. You shouldn't cause too much trouble."

A slight semblance of order had been restored within the classroom. At least the new particles that kept appearing found their assigned seats quickly. He decided that he could start the lesson.

"Today I am going to lecture," Jonathan began, "on neutrino and antineutrino etiquette. Whenever one of you heavier particles decides to decay into a lepton and a neutrino, it can't be just *any* neutrino. Remember that it's not polite if the neutrino type doesn't match the lepton type! The same rule holds if you've decided to collide with a neutrino. If you want to make an electron, make sure that it's an electron neutrino you're running into, unless you want to make a subatomic faux pas. Also if you collide with a neutrino, you must produce a negatively charged lepton. If it's an antineutrino, you must make antimatter – a positively charged lepton. It's the opposite if you are decaying into a lepton and a neutrino or antineutrino. Negatively charged leptons will then go with antineutrinos, positively charged ones with neutrinos. Antineutrino types are matched with lepton types just like neutrinos are. It's necessary if you want to make a good impression." Jonathan paused for a moment. "Are there any questions?"

"I've got a question," a positive sigma piped up. "Why do *we* need to know all of these rules? We are not even leptons and the rules are so boring!"

"Boring! I'll teach you to give me any backtalk! In fact...um...where did he go?

"We don't know, Mr. Electron," a neutral lambda said. "He was here just ten to the minus ten seconds ago."

"Well, ask them!" He pointed to a proton and a neutral pion that had suddenly appeared. "He produced them. Maybe they know."

"We don't!" they protested. "Honest."

"Not only are you unruly," said Jonathan, "but you won't even help me find and punish the troublemakers!"

At this, the class, insulted, left their assigned seats. The scores of new particles sat wherever they felt like, despite Jonathan Electron's protests. While yelling at his students, he was nearly hit by an electron antineutrino from a neutron beta decay. That was the last straw.

"All right!" he cried. "I am sending all of you to Principal Proton!"

"No, you can't send us!" replied the young protons. "We're positively charged like he is. We'll fly right back out of his office."

"Do you really think that I am stupid?" Jonathan shot back. "You're forgetting...the strong force!"

"We're in trouble now!" yelled the distraught protons.

Jonathan got on the intercom. "Hello, this is Mr. Electron. Send the gluon patrol to room 12. I need some unruly protons brought to the principal. Oh, and some neutrons too." The neutrons blanched along with the protons.

"What can you do to us?" the leptons having mass asked him. "We don't feel the strong force!"

"True, you don't. But you can't escape gravity!" He got on the intercom again. "Send a squad of gravitons to room 12. They're to bring trouble making electrons, muons and taus to Principal Proton."

"You might have gotten them," A muon neutrino said. "But we neutrinos can't be taken by gluons or gravitons." How will you get us to the Principal?"

"I won't. You won't be able to get into mischief if it's just you neutrinos in the room. Being away from the other particles for a while ought to teach you a lesson." (As smart as Jonathan was, he forgot that the antineutrinos were also there. They and the neutrinos once left alone could play around and produce all kinds of new particles if they could get energized, but that is another story.)

The gluon patrol and the graviton squad restored order for the moment, but Principal Proton reminded Jonathan after class that it is simply the nature of most subatomic particles to decay and collide. Jonathan mulled over his superiors words and decided that he was not right for this teaching assignment. He was not cut out, after all, to instruct such unruly students. He had been wrong to desire more challenge in his work, Jonathan thought to himself. He returned to Mediator High and his gravitons, happy to once again teach simple particles in peace.

THE CASE OF PARTICLE X
BY MATT TAIT (1995)
MUSIC MAJOR

Around Precinct 10^{-10}, the fuzz got plenty of calls about things missing; a proton getting his stereo jacked or a neutron losing his wallet on the subway. Sometimes, a cracked radium nucleus –"unstable," the doctors called it– would flip for a while and when it came to it would have a couple protons and neutrons missing. Course then; it wasn't a radium nucleus anymore. So Detective Cern thought he'd seen it all when Lieutenant Fermi called from downtown.

"Cern, we gotta problem. A carbon nuclei busted up right into two."

"What kinda problem is that? If you called me for every alpha or gamma bust-up, I'd…"

"Save it, Cern. This one's diffcrent. Real different. It's even got the commissioner worried. Get down here pronto."

Cern drove to the downtown station puzzled all right. A particle decay was about as criminal an activity as tying your shoe. He stepped out of his cruiser and let Fermi brief him.

"Lemme get this straight. We got seven protons." He glanced over at one end of the interrogation room, and gave the group a once-over. Pretty chipper particles for an investigation. What'd he expect from positive particles. "We got seven neutrons." They were in the middle of the room, not too frazzled: not too happy, either. "And one electron." There was the single electron, looking depressed. No surprises.

"Yeah, Fermi, so it looks like the particles didn't get separately conserved. Big deal. Looks to me like one neutron –since there are eight in a carbon atom–busted up into a proton and an electron. So now instead of six protons and eight neutrons, we got seven, seven, and a new electron. A little weird, but it makes sense."

"Alright, smart guy," said Fermi, "then explain where the proton's sitting."

Fermi was right–something was wrong. Dead wrong. If this was your everyday reaction, the electron would've been sitting directly opposite one of the protons–they were naturally repulsed; who knew why. But this one sat off at an angle from his corresponding proton. Cern saw the problem. Time to play the bad cop. It came natural to him.

He stormed over to the electron. "We got laws around here, pal. Law of Conservation of Momentum. Ring any bells?"

"Well of course it does," moped the electron.

"Well then what's the big idea? If you're gonna bust up from a neutron into a proton and an electron, you gotta bust up back-to-back. Know why? 'Cause that means the sum of your masses times velocities are equal, and that means you're conserving momentum."

"Obviously," he snipped, "I know all this. That's why me and the other particles called you. We're missing some energy. Somebody stole it from us."

Fermi took him aside. "I know liars, Cern, and none of these guys are lying. We got two parties missing some energy, and nobody here's hiding it. Our particle–the thief particle–is still on the loose."

Back in the cruiser, Cern tried to make sense of it. No footprints for a Particle X: no eyewitness accounts of him, either. And if you have mass, you leave footprints, and if you got a charge, another particle gets sucked your way or the other way, and if you don't got either, you ain't no particle. Yup. Real puzzled. And then the radio shrieked. Fermi at the other end.

"Cern, we just got a tip. A gang– they call themselves Weak Force–has a rat. I gave him a couple bucks, and he sang. Says his crew's gotta contract. They help another gang, The Tiny Neutral Ones, perpetrate just the kinda crime we're lookin' at. But the deal is real exclusive-like. They don't have nothin' to do with bust-ups unless the bustups have somethin' to do with The Tiny Neutral Ones. So he knows 'em real well, and he says they all gots no mass, and no charge. And he helped out with our crime –I don't know just how yet–but he gave me names. He got two guys mighta done it. Sure is tough tellin' 'em apart, though. Come on

12

back downtown. If I can't get a positive I.D., I will need a confession, and if I need a confession, I need a bad cop. You're it."

He turned around and headed back downtown. So now he had some more answers, but more questions to match. What kinda guys had no mass and no charge? What kinda gangs call themselves "Weak Force" and "Tiny Neutral Ones?" Come to think of it, he'd heard about that Weak Force bunch a while back. Heard there were three types of Weak Forcers. All that made 'em real confusing and a whole lot shadier than the boys in the Strong, Electro, or Gravitational packs. Didn't trust 'em. Least the other boys kept it simple–one gang, one type.

When Cern got back to the precinct, Fermi had two particles behind a two-way mirror. He also had something to go on.

"One of 'em is real nervous–doesn't want the crime to get pinned on him–and he's singin' like a bird. Telling us all about his group–call themselves the neutrinos, I guess– and their rules. Said something about how they won't have nothing to do with the strange particles; that they only pop out when protons and neutrons bust up. I don't think that info helps us any. He also says that they have a rule about something called lepton number. He says since he's a neutrino, and not an antineutrino, his lepton number is +1. And since the rules that govern the street say that the total number of lepton particles before a reaction has to equal to the number of those after a reaction, he couldn't have been in the bust-up, and couldn't have made off with any extra energy. The neutron's lepton number is 0, see, and the particles after the bust-up, which include a neutrino and an electron, which also has a lepton charge of +1, as well as a proton–lepton number of 0–would have a total lepton number of 2. So our rule about lepton number being equal before and after the bust up is broken, see? So it really can't be him."

"I follow you," said Cern. "But if it was the antineutrino, his lepton number, -1, would cancel out the electron's + 1, and bingo, you have an equation with equal sides. One problem . . ." he glanced through the reflective window. "How do we tell them apart?"

"Tough one. If they're an antiparticle pair like they say they are, that means they're the same. No opposite value exists for 0 mass; no opposite property exists for neutral charge, and their spin is the same. So maybe you can make 'em talk."

An hour later, Cern emerged from the interrogation room.

"You make 'em talk?" asked Fermi.

"Yeah. We had one clever criminal in there–only he's no criminal at all."

"You're making about as much sense as this case, and that's none."

"Wrong, Fermi. That's a lot. It's simple. The other particle–the one who wasn't talking before–got scared and said that there was some stuff the other guy wasn't telling me. That the rules the first guy told me were true, but that also he, and the other guy, were different. Seems they got this quality called spin. It's inside 'em. Not visible from the outside. So I called in a specialist, and sure enough, they were different. The first guy to talk–said he was a neutrino at first, remember–was spinning one way. The specialist said that made him an antineutrino, and that made him, by the rules he explained to us, guilty. He was the only particle that could've been in the bust up. But, clever guy, he tried to pin his identity on the other particle who was spinning the wrong way. So that guy was the real neutrino, and so he couldn't have been at the bust up, or lepton number wouldn't have been conserved."

"Good work. So what do we charge them with?"

"Like I said, he's no criminal. If he wasn't around, how else could we account for the missing energy in today's carbon bust-up? Forget theft. I say we charge him with upholding the Law of Energy Conservation.

"Real good work, Cern."

MY NAME IS ATOM
BY AMANDA MCBAINE (1992)
ART MAJOR

One day, a short old man with a quizzical face approached me, dragging a suitcase behind him. Scared at first, having lived my life in the sanctity and solitude of my own world, a world in which I was free to run naked and do what I like, I ran to hide, but soon realized the man was blind. He could not see anything, so I could rest easy. I was a mystery to him. As much as I tried to hide, this was the beginning of a long relationship, a game if you will, through the course of which this man and I have gone through a lot. He explained to me that first day that he was curious about me, that he wanted to get to know me, to know of my world and what I looked like, that in fact he would like to play a game with me, if I would be so obliged. The game was to answer his question, "What was I?" He then showed me the game tools he had brought with him in his bag, most of which looked fairly harmless to me, and anyway, the man was blind, so I needn't worry, I was going to win this game, and preserve my mystery. I was invisible.

Because the poor man couldn't use his eyes, his tools for this discovery game were his hands. I laughed the first time he tried to feel the structure of my face because I knew this wasn't going to get him anywhere. He said to me, "You are made of water, I know, though you try to evade me by changing states and tricking my hands!" Satisfied, he closed his suitcase and sat upon it, quietly for a long, long time.

As the years passed the question mark on his face became more pronounced. One day he came running back to me yelling something about how I wasn't only made of water, in fact, the air, fire and earth were all part of my domain too. True enough, I thought, but it didn't scare me. He was still far from winning the game. It wasn't till many years after that, that the man began to scare me. It was then that he said to me, "You are just one, of many uncuttable things, that make up the air, fire, water and earth. You are very little, and it is not just because I am blind and handicapped that you are winning this game. Even if I did have eyes, you are cunning and would hide." He was gaining on me but it was a while before I would have to worry, just until he began using his game tools.

Again, the man sat quietly on his suitcase for many years. One day however, a furious rage hit him and he began scratching diagrams and pictures onto a piece of paper from within his bag. He showed it to me calling it 'The Periodic Table'. He told me that I was not alone, and that in fact there were many different kinds of me. Many types of invisible, cunning things, in varying forms, made up the world. The next move he made was to shoot radioactive elements at me, screaming to himself that he was the 'Curator' or 'Curieur' or something. I cannot remember. He then felt my face again with his delicate fingers. "You are not what you seem, my friend, alas you have more than just a face, you are made of distinct features. What is inside you is more essential than you yourself." Uh-oh, the man was surprisingly perceptive for being blind and all. The notion of what was I, in particular, what was I made of, poisoned the old man for the next hundred years. He found a new strategy in the game, and he required many instruments. A few years later he put a 'scintillating' screen behind me (he always used such funny words!) and gave me a shove till I hit the screen. But lucky me, I came out the other side. Somehow he had managed to take an abstract picture of me, which I found thoroughly annoying. He felt my face again, and smiling, said, " I've got it. You look like plum pudding. In my mind I can see that your face is mostly positive substance, but that there are raisin bits of negative substance floating around. You are two parts." Whatever I thought; this man was either crazy or hungry.

His next move was slightly saner though as he stopped trying to superimpose his world onto mine. Calling himself Einstein or Planck (he could not make up his mind), he devised a new theory about me and my good looks. He said I was like a galaxy, still made of two parts, one that orbited and one that was orbited, a much more flattering idea than plum pudding if you ask me. "Electrons that orbited and a nucleus around which they orbited," said Rutherford. Again, he had changed his name.

Again he went back to his drawing board, feverishly sketched for a while, rummaged through his suitcase and swore a bit. Then haggard, but more alive than ever with curiosity sustaining him, he charged back at me armed with the same polonium stuff he had used before. But much to my surprise, his intentions were much different. After he shot an alpha radiator gun at me, I was shoved though a screen of Beryllium, I lost my ears, my electrons, in his funny terminology, at which point I then hit another blockade of paraffin in which my nose was lodged. Only my eyes were left coming out the other side. He immediately ran to feel my face and quickly realized that in fact I was only eyes now and that I had in fact three parts to my face. He, I should tell you that his name is now Chadwick, called them, electron, neutron, and proton. Well, this was not the same kind of game that I was told about in the very beginning, when the man called himself Thales, and all his instruments were harmless. Not only had he changed names, but this game was now without a doubt harmful. No one likes having her face ripped apart. This didn't seem to bother the man though, and little did I know that his plans for harming me would escalate in the future.

The day he discovered my mouth (he called it the little neutral one) was the day I began to understand that in fact, he might win this game. The powers of his tools were of great advantage to him, and despite being blind, he could still sort of see. The tools he pulled out of his bag became larger, more complex, and worst of all, more destructive. Just take my mouth for instance, had it not been for what he called his, Savanna River Nuclear Reactor, I could never have been contained, or 'seen' (in as much as he can see).

The man just wasn't kidding when he said he wanted to get to know me. Had I ever been told that a blind man could still build tools to see, and that his mind was capable of thinking things outside of his world and in mine, I never would have agreed to play. Just in the last hundred years, the man has tripled his capability to build machines, change his name, and understand my world. He has even bothered many friends of mine in the process of figuring me out, giving them equally monstrous names of leptons, photons, gluons, gravitons and bosons. By forcing them to reveal information using his power of coercion aided by his big machines, he has begun to understand the relationships in our world. He even bothered my heavy friend omega, a dangerous fellow; what nerve!

The most frightening part by far is the fact that his understanding presupposes his discovery, which leads me to believe that his mind is by far the most dangerous of his tools. Take for example, his figuring of the skeletal structure of my face. Finnegan was his name at that point and sub-structure was his game. He was no longer feeling my face for its surface beauty but decided that what lay underneath was far more important. It was long before he could 'see' my skeleton that he knew it was there. Unhappily he called my bones, 'quarks'. But again, I was powerless to defend myself; he had me contained. He had by now exposed my eyes, my nose, my ears, my bones, my friends, and all of our relationships. Many of my friends are now incarcerated in large machines where they are forced to hit one another at high speeds, just for the sake of being 'seen'.

That is our story, the man and I. Although it sounds like a losing battle, inevitably to be won by the man, I still have hope. Though my friends and I are torn apart day, by day, we never die. Can the same be said of the man? Will curiosity kill him? You see, the fact is, that though he can build many machines, and his mind can grow pregnant with big ideas, he still has a handicap; he is blind. He will never see our world. We are invisible, and that is our eternal mystery.

JAIL BREAK
BY BASIM AL-HADDAD (1995)
HISTORY MAJOR

Billy D. Electron, inmate number 3141592654, was tired of jail. He had served two years of a ten-year sentence for a crime he did not commit. He had been falsely charged and convicted because he did not have any rights; he was an immigrant in a land of protons. Life in jail was too much. He was constantly being harassed by the prison guards as well as by other inmates. He had had enough and decided to get out. But before the story can go on, we must go back to a cold winter's night two years earlier in which Billy D's life changed forever in the xenophobic land of protons.

Billy was a stranger in a strange land. He was living in a country dominated by the proton race. It was impossible for him to fit in and his co-workers always made fun of him because his mass was smaller than that of protons and because his charge was negative instead of positive like the proton majority. It was hard to find solace in such a hateful environment, but Billy was not alone.

One cold winter night he was walking home after work with his neutron friend Tammy, who was also an immigrant. They were laughing, trying to make light of the repressive state of their lives in Protonland when a drunken bunch of protons attacked then. The police soon arrived, and the protons claimed that they were trying to make a citizen's arrest. The leader of the group told the police officers that Billy and Tammy had been trying to produce a reaction that did not conserve charge. This was a serious accusation because there was a law that prohibited particles from participating in reactions where charge was not conserved. The police, without hesitation, arrested Billy and Tammy and took them to the station for booking. On the day of Billy's trial, he was convicted. The only evidence offered against him was the word of the protons with whom he had had the altercation.

Over the next two years Billy had grown weary of attempting to use legal means, such as appeals, to get out of jail. He decided that the only way left was for him to escape. But how? He had tried to break through the wall by running and increasing his velocity (accelerating himself). He hoped that this increase in his velocity would increase his kinetic energy, and if this happened, his total energy would have a corresponding increase. In turn, he would be able to exert enough force on the wall to create a hole big enough for him to escape. However, accelerating himself simply by running did not allow him to reach an energy level high enough for him to break through because his mass was too low. One day, however, Billy D. had a great idea.

He was sitting in his room on a Tuesday afternoon when all of a sudden his Walkman stopped working. He looked to see if the light that indicated the batteries were dead was on. Sure enough it was. He got off of his bed and went to check his drawer for extra batteries, but he was out. At that moment he saw a guard walk by and asked him if he could have extra batteries. The guard responded, "You know the rules smally (in prison all of the protons referred to the electrons as smally because of their smaller mass), only one set of batteries a week!" His neighbor heard his request and after the guard left offered to trade his batteries for Billy's cigarettes. Billy agreed. He then had a great idea. He would collect batteries by trading things he did not need with other inmates for their batteries. Once he had collected enough batteries he could build an accelerator to help him to break out of prison.

Over the next year Billy traded items that he received, such as cigarettes, candy, gum, and magazines, with other inmates for their batteries. At the end of the year, Billy had collected over 520 batteries (he collected around 10 a week over the 52 week period). He also needed metal plates, one for each positive and negative side of the battery. He made these plates himself in the prison's metal shop where he worked. Once he had collected enough batteries and metal plates, he decided that he was ready to build a linear accelerator powerful enough for his needs.

He set out to find an area around the prison long enough for him to set up his accelerator. He located the perfect place next to one of the prison walls. Once he found the needed area he started to build his accelerator at night in his room. Every morning he would store each section of his accelerator in a drainage ditch that ran under and parallel to the prison wall.

One night, after the 11:00 P.M. role call, he was able to sneak out of his cell and onto the prison lawn. He made his way to the wall where he had stored the parts to his accelerator and proceeded to set it up. He knew that he had to have it operating before 5:00 A.M. because the guards would check the grounds at that time. He was successful and had the accelerator ready by 4:30 A.M.

His accelerator worked in the following manner. The metal plates that were connected to the positive and negative ends of each battery created an electric field in the gap between them. The direction of the electric field went south and his desired point of exit was north. Thus he would have to enter at the southern point. Once Billy entered the first field he would experience a force and be accelerated in the direction opposite to the field (because he had a negative charge) sending him into the next field. He hoped that he had built enough fields to allow for the succession of small voltages to boost him to higher and higher energy levels. He would soon find out.

At 4:35 Billy entered the first field. The force of the field accelerated him in the direction opposite of the field (from south to north which was what he wanted), and his velocity increased in that same direction. He was then sent through the next field and then the next. At the end of each acceleration his velocity increased which resulted in an increase in his energy. By the time Billy exited his accelerator he had a speed almost equal to the speed of light. The increase in energy allowed him to hit the wall with a great force, creating a hole for him to exit (of course he was wearing a helmet for protection).

Billy D. was free. He vowed never again to let the protons catch him. He went off into the uncertain abyss and no one really knows where he is today.

Stories

22

CRISIS MEDIATION
BY MICHAEL A. BENEDETTO (1997)
COGNITIVE SCIENCE MAJOR

George Gluon sighed in exhaustion. "I'd almost rather see this happy nucleus fall apart than continue listening to them whine," he thought grumpily. He shook his head (at least, what he liked to think of as a head). "No, I've got to try and do some good here. I'm a strong force mediator, and it's my job. I'll see if throwing my weight around does any good."

He started to speak, and then remembered that he had no mass to speak of (or charge, for that matter). No wonder the particles he dealt with found him so easy to ignore. They paused for a microsecond, and then went on with what they were saying. George wished that he could tamper with their internal compositions, and perhaps change their quark types and make them a little bit easier to deal with. He shook his head (?) again. No, that would be weak.

"I just feel like I'm going in circles, and I haven't even been in that damned accelerator for a while," wailed Paula Proton. "I'm so conflicted, Doctor. There are forces pulling us in every direction—the strong force is holding us together, the electromagnetic force is pulling us apart—and I just don't know which way to spin anymore."

"Wait a minute," George interrupted. "What do you know about the electromagnetic force?"

Paula looked a bit sheepish. "I've been seeing this mediator on the side. Do you know Pamela Photon? She's extraordinary; she has an infinite range. Anyway, she's been telling me that positively charged particles are just no good for me; that I've got to free myself of this nucleus and find myself a nice single electron. And to tell you the truth, I think she makes a lot of sense."

George shook his head—well, never mind—in exasperation. He knew Pamela, all right. Her range was indeed infinite—her price range, that is. The protons must be doing very well if they could afford her services as well as his own. "Paula, I don't think an electromagnetic force mediator can provide quite what you're looking for."

"Yeah, you tell her, Doc," interrupted Peter Proton. "That witch is just out to get me. Pure particleism, I tell you."

"Quiet, Peter," George instructed. "You may not realize it now, Paula, but the electromagnetic force gets weaker the more distance there is between the two of you. So if you were ever to go off on your own, you would no longer feel repelled by him. What's more, the strong force works in the opposite way—just as the quarks within you have incredible difficulty in moving too far apart, you would have incredible difficulty in leaving the nucleus. Would that make a difference to you?"

"Oh, dear," sighed Paula. "Yes, I suppose that it would."

Nancy Neutron groaned audibly, as she had heard this all before. "Can we go home now? This has nothing to do with me."

"This has everything to do with you, young lady," retorted Peter. "We are trying to keep this atom from coming apart, and you are going to stay here and work with us."

Nancy snorted. "I've been seeing a mediator too."

George's heart (or something like that) sank.

"And he says that I could do a lot better than being just some neutron. I mean, one up quark and two downs; that's small potatoes!"

George decided to take a sensible approach. "What do you want to be, Nancy?"

"Well, my atomic clock is ticking like crazy. Neutrons only live about 930 seconds, you know. I want to go crazy, live life to the fullest, and explore my inner strangeness, which I certainly can't do here."

"Her inner strangeness, she says!" moaned Paula. "Nancy, you're a neutron! You have no strangeness!"

"You see what I mean?" Nancy replied. "They're stifling me. I have to get out of this nucleus pronto. My mediator wants to make me into a proton. I'll live for over 10^{30} years, and I'll be a lot more attractive, that's for sure."

"And who would your mediator be?" asked George, who had a feeling that he already knew.

"That would be me," a voice called from the doorway. It was Will W. (short for W minus), George's archenemy and a known weak force mediator. "Through my revolutionary technique of beta decay, Nancy will be a beautiful, healthy proton. I came here to see what you plan to do about it."

"What I plan to do about it?" repeated George. "I don't plan to do anything whatsoever."

"Doctor!" exclaimed both Peter and Paula.

"Though I personally would never stoop to the actual transformation of a quark within a patient, I recognize Nancy's right to disagree and seek help elsewhere." Nancy, surprised, began to show some interest in what he was saying.

"Let this be a test for all of you," he continued. "If you really feel that you would be better off going your separate ways, then by all means do so. If not, however..."

He paused dramatically, and all of the other particles leaned in closer. He began again, only to be immediately interrupted by soft music coming through the loudspeaker. "Oh, I'm afraid our time is up for today. We'll start from there next week, that is, assuming that you're all willing to be here."

The nucleons all nodded enthusiastically. Will grumbled, but said nothing. "Good!" George continued. "Take care, then."

As the particles drifted out, George thought to himself, "They don't call this the strong force for nothing."

PRINCESS ZUZU
BY JOHN J. MONTESSA (1990)
LATIN MAJOR

Once upon a time, there was a subatomic kingdom called Atomica, which was the size of a pinhead. It was a beautiful kingdom and its inhabitants basked in the glory of its ample abundance. The citizens were content living here for the many nanoseconds of their lives and they revered the sovereign who protected and provided them with great benevolence. King Pomp, himself a proton, loved his people a great deal and showed them his love by maintaining order in the kingdom by overseeing all the reactions in it. This was his duty for he and his kingdom were loyal to the great god, Conservation.

In ancient times, the kingdom knew nothing but chaos because the reactions that took place had neither rhyme nor reason. One day, King Pomp's great, great, great grandfather, King Baffle, was walking in the subatomic forest, brooding about the utter anarchy which was now dominating his realm, when suddenly he saw a bright light. He fell down and cowered on the ground certain that he was being punished for being unable to maintain order in the kingdom.

"I don't know who you are or what you want, but please have mercy," King Baffle pleaded.

"King Baffle, your kingdom is great and I have come to help you save it." The light responded sagaciously.

The king was circumspect at first but he eventually overcame his initial fear and listened to the light who he learned was the god Conservation, incognito of course. They conversed for many hours and King Baffle learned the sacred Conservation laws of Charge, Momentum, Baryon Number, Energy, and Strangeness, which were etched upon a stone tablet that the god provided. King Baffle took the commandments back to the castle and later enforced them throughout the kingdom.

From then on the great kingdom of Atomica knew peace and serenity just because of these Commandments of

Conservation, which enabled the reactions to happen without creating chaos.

Some inhabitants were so impressed by Conservation that they spent their lives worshipping him. As a result they were given even deeper knowledge of their own universe. They became saints when they died. Among them were Dirac, Rutherford, and Einstein.

Conservation, himself, had a special place in his heart for King Baffle for having the good sense to listen to him. As a result, the god promised King Baffle and his descendents good fortune and happiness in the forthcoming epochs as long as they remained loyal.

However, regardless of the god's special benediction, one descendent knew the horrors of melancholy. This unhappy proton was Zuzu, the only daughter of King Pomp. No one could understand her unhappiness since she was beautiful, intelligent, and the daughter of the king of Atomica. Even stranger was the fact that she would become queen of Atomica when her father stepped down. Surely a proton this fortunate would be able to find something to make her happy. Yet, gloom prevailed.

King Pomp tried everything to make his poor Zuzu happy but all endeavors were in vain. Her ever-present frown was an aberration in the happy kingdom of Atomica. As a final recourse, King Pomp appealed to his people advocating the happiness of his daughter. He declared that whomever could make her happy would win a large portion of the royal treasury.

So everyone tried to make her happy. A great line of people stretched from the castle as far as the eye could see. Everyone, eager for the great reward, attempted to make the otherwise unhappy princess happy with sundry stunts intended to inspire mirth. Zuzu saw everything from jugglers and clowns to poets and singers. Yet, no one was successful. She also heard a host of jokes from various citizens. However, each joke was a failure, even the joke about the muon, the pion, and the lambda that walked into a subatomic bar. Needless to say, King Baffle was worried.

While the contest went on at the castle, a young neutron named Bosco roamed the subatomic forest. He wasn't at the contest because he knew nothing about it since he had been wandering the forest for many milliseconds wallowing in his grief from the lack of true love. This deficiency had in fact made him a little crazy. His appearance was rather disturbing because his clothing was tattered and soiled by the elements and his face was tearstained from crying, which he did often. He also moaned and groaned like a spectre doomed to suffering for an eternity. Undisputedly, Bosco was a pathetic sight.

Bosco was carrying on as he usually did when suddenly a bright light appeared above. It was Conservation, who had come to alleviate this poor neutron's misery. Bosco looked up and thought that his death was certain but he wasn't frightened.

Instead, he yelled with insolence, "I don't know who you are or what you want, but if you have come to kill me, please be swift for I have suffered for what seems like an eternity."

"Why should I kill you? I am Conservation the Merciful. I have come to help you," the god responded.

Bosco stood in utter consternation. He thought that since he couldn't find his true love, he was unworthy of it. Since he was unworthy of love, he was certain he was worthy of death. "Please, great Conservation, end my pathetic existence," he pleaded.

"No, you are miserable and no one else in Atomica is unhappy except for one other than yourself. You must go to her for it is destined," the god said adamantly.

"Where can I find her?" Bosco asked between sobs.

"At the castle. Go there and you will find what you are looking for." As Conservation said this, the light slowly faded away.

Hearing the orders of the god, Bosco decided to walk to the castle. However, being a born pessimist, he was doubtful, so he continued crying and moaning as he slowly made his way.

Meanwhile, at the castle, the line was getting shorter and shorter as everyone filed through the royal court trying to make Zuzu laugh. Still, no one had been successful. The princess remained stoic as a monk unaffected by the citizens' attempts.

At sunset, Bosco finally reached the castle tired and miserable. The line was very short now as Bosco walked into the castle. The guards and the citizens looked at him as if he was a basilisk and they didn't attempt to stop him. Everyone just stared at him because he looked so horrible. All the while Bosco sobbed as he made his way into the royal court where King Pomp, his royal entourage, and Princess Zuzu were sitting. The princess was bored from hours of uninteresting entertainment.

The king, who was by now irritable after seeing the antics of so many talentless hacks, saw Bosco and said, "Goodness, what a vile and disgusting excuse for a citizen of Atomica. Really, I should have the guard who let that in sent to the collider."

"I've been sent by the great god Conservation," Bosco replied.

"Goodness, A blaspheme! Why would our god speak to you, being as repugnant as you are? Guards, take this particle to the collider!"

The guards at their king's bidding, hurried toward Bosco, brandishing clubs. They caught Bosco and dragged him away from the court, nearly tearing all the tatters off his already exposed body. Bosco struggled and soon gave up, once again miserable. Abruptly, he fell to the floor beneath the guards and began crying uncontrollably. The atmosphere was completely chaotic and well, embarrassing.

All of a sudden laughter filled the great hall and echoed throughout the castle. Everyone looked around for its source. Finally, everyone's eyes fixed upon Princess Zuzu for she was laughing aloud unreservedly. She had seen this strange looking particle wrestled and beaten by the guards and then watched as he sobbed half-naked and prostrate on the floor. She was unable to control her laughter.

Bosco looked up to see who it was that was laughing and saw the most beautiful particle he had ever beheld. Cupid had shot his gluons and he found himself drawn to Princess Zuzu. He had finally found his true love. The princess was also intrigued by this most unusual neutron and found that she too was struck by Cupid's gluons. A smile graced both their faces as they looked at each other.

King Pomp was overwhelmed with happiness because his daughter was finally happy and in turn his tender disposition returned. He announced that Bosco was the winner of the contest and would receive part of the royal treasury.

It was love at first sight and Bosco and Zuzu were married, bound by a strong force. The great god, Conservation, had after all kept his promise to the family of King Baffle by ensuring the happiness of Princess Zuzu. After King Pomp stepped down many milliseconds later, Bosco and Zuzu became the king and queen of Atomica, where they lived happily ever after.

Stories

THE MIDLIFE CRISIS OF TONY PROTON
BY JENNIFER M. ALLEN (2002)
PSYCHOLOGY MAJOR

Hello! My name is Tony. I am a proton. I would like to tell you a story about a problem I had a little while back and how it got fixed. Hopefully, some of you out there will learn from my experience without having to go through it the hard way like I did. So, here goes.

Having been alive for about 10,000,000,000,000,000 years, things were looking kind of bleak for me. I was not even halfway through my existence on this planet and so far, my life could be described as rather mundane. Ask anyone—I had an extremely stable personality. All the other particles could count on me to be around when they needed me. I was always positive—a really upbeat personality. But after a while, this cheerfulness was feeling a bit fake. I was craving excitement—any kind of change, really. I was even a little envious of the smaller particles like the pions and muons. They had really short lifetimes, which meant that they had to make a point of living during the time they had to the fullest. I just did not feel that kind of motivation. How could I? I was facing thousands upon thousands more years of the "same old same old."

Clearly, I had a bit of a problem. I had to do something to make my life feel like it was worth living. For a bit of a change of scenery, I decided to become a part of a hydrogen atom that was going to be in a water molecule. I thought the constant change in state might help liven things up for me. For a while, this did work. It was rather exciting to be in an ocean one day, in a cloud another day, and then end up in an iceberg. I got to see quite a bit of the world as part of the water molecule. Unfortunately, everything gets old after a while. After about 600 years of this world traveling that I was doing, I started to get bored again. When it finally got to the point where I could not bear the thought of being sent to a glacier in Canada again, I escaped my water molecule.

So, I wandered around aimlessly for a good amount of time, feeling gloomier and gloomier as each day passed. After a while, I guess I began to grate on the nerves of my fellow protons. I just was not fitting in with them. Instead of being happy and exhibiting a positive personality like everyone else, I was beginning to give off negative vibes. Finally, the other protons suggested that I might be better off finding protons more like myself. I guess what they really meant was that they were getting tired of my negativity. So away I went.

I had heard talk of a very strange group of protons. They called themselves antiprotons. They looked just like us regular protons—they had the same mass and spins as us. The only difference was that they had very negative personalities. And this negativity did not just come from depression—they were born that way! I decided to go and see if they might be a group that I would want to join.

After much searching, I finally found a group of antiprotons in a town called Geneva in Switzerland. They lived in a thing called a collider named CERN. I should have realized right away that there was something odd about the whole situation, but I was not seeing past my personal crisis. As I talked to these antiprotons, they seemed more and more appealing. They were very excited to see me, and wanted me to join their group. As an initiation, they wanted me to get into this great big machine and get propelled in a circle faster and faster and faster. That sounded kind of interesting, but I did not see much point to the activity. After more questioning, I found out that they wanted me to bump into one of them during one of these fast circles. This was when I realized that something was really wrong with these guys.

It turned out that this was a self-destructive, kamikaze group of particles. Actually, their sole purpose for existence was to annihilate themselves with protons. They were not even natural particles—they were created by scientists! Their job was to convince unsuspecting protons to join their "club" by entering this collider. Now, if I was a younger proton, I might have fallen for this. Luckily, though, 10,000,000,000,000,000 years gives a particle plenty of time to get to know his inner self. I was fully aware that I was made up of three little things called quarks—two up quarks and one down quark. If I agreed to smash into one of the antiprotons, these quarks could very possibly have been set free. As far as I knew, they would not be able to survive off on their own. They needed me! Also, if I agreed to this crazy scheme, what would become of me? I had been bored with my life, but certainly not bored enough to purposely annihilate myself forever!

Well, this was just the wake-up call I needed. A stable, predictable life was better than none at all! I could not be so selfish. I had to consider the needs of the tiny particles living inside me—if they were good enough to stay together so that I could be alive, then I owed it to them to remain in existence so that *they* could live. As you can see, we had sort of a mutual-dependency relationship going on here. Considering all this, it was an easy decision to make. I high-tailed it out of the vicinity of those evil antiprotons. They certainly were *anti*-protons—they wanted to cause protons to cease existence!

So, that is my story. I learned a very tough lesson—even a mundane, highly predictable life is worth living. It took a brush with total annihilation to help me see that. Sometimes I wonder, though. I did not want to join the antiproton "club" because I was afraid of the unknown. Who knows—maybe annihilation would not have meant nonexistence. Maybe it would have put me on a whole other plane of existence. I don't have to think about that right now, though. I have quite a few more years to live a happy, positive life. I know where to find those antiprotons. Maybe I will be ready to be adventurous when I am closer to the end of my long, long life. So come see what I am up to in another several thousand (or million or billion) years. Maybe I'll have a different attitude about this whole business…

Stories

LUCY AND THE PARTICLE COLLIDER
BY ALYSSA BABCOCK (1995)
CHEMISTRY MAJOR

"Look out! We're being collected!"

The helium atoms scattered to avoid the physicists. Lucy the proton stayed still, excited and expectant. Today was her lucky day. She was pretty sure that she was going to be put into a particle accelerator. She had heard her parents speaking in hushed tones about how her cousin Mika had been collected and had turned into a strange quark. Lucy wasn't surprised. Mika had been a bizarre proton. Her sister, Caroline, had ended up in a helium balloon for some little kid. Lucy smiled. She knew she might see her again someday, and, oh, wouldn't Caroline be surprised if Lucy had turned into a top quark!! The thought made her giggle with happiness.

The ride to the accelerator wasn't too bad. The accelerator, though, turned out to be vast and menacing like a large coil of snake. There was an ominous detection center of some sort, but Lucy couldn't quite see it. She cried out as she was separated from her atom and put into a large box. It was there that she met Andrew. Andrew was a proton too. He smiled at Lucy.

"Are you ready?" he asked kindly.

"Oh, Yes!" squealed Lucy.

"We're going to smash, you know."

"I know," said Lucy. "My cousin came out as a strange quark!"

What do you think we'll turn into?" mused Andrew.

"They want a top quark, I heard. They haven't got enough evidence to prove their existence yet. I don't know exactly how it works."

Andrew laughed. "I heard that they smash us into antiprotons. Imagine that!"

"Really? But there hasn't been any antimatter since the Great War. My grandfather told me he saw the last of the antimatter die on the battlefield. He was such a brave proton."

"I don't know," interrupted Andrew. "Perhaps they make it somehow."

"Yes, that must be it. I wonder how. You know, most protons would be afraid of antimatter, but for some reason I'm not. I'm actually rather excited. Oh, Andrew, what if we turn into top quarks?"

"I doubt we will. They've only seen six so far."

There was a really loud noise as the group ahead of them was sent off into the large tube. Lucy didn't know how they were supposed to fly around the tube. She could fly, but not that quickly, not quickly enough to turn her energy into a Top Quark. She fell silent. She heard the faraway smash of protons and antiprotons.

"Hey Lucy, why the long face?" asked Andrew. " I thought you were excited."

"I am," said Lucy. "Only I was just thinking, I don't know if I can fly that fast."

"Well," said Andrew. "I guess we'll find out in a minute, cause it's our turn now."

It was the loudest sound they had ever heard. They were suddenly surrounded by the vast tube, and flying at a dizzying speed.

" But I'm not flying this fast!" said Lucy. "In fact, I'm not flying at all!"

"I think it's from the magnets," said Andrew decisively. "I can feel them sort of pulling at me, making us go faster."

"Me too!" said Lucy. She suddenly laughed and unexpectedly broke into song. "It's so stupendous, living in this tube"

Andrew joined the song. "Living in this tuuuube …"

"Hey!" giggled Lucy. "That's good!"

"So stupendous..." belted Lucy.

A nasty looking proton turned around and told her to shut up or he'd bash her up quarks out. Lucy stuck out her tongue at the other proton and looked at Andrew sheepishly. He was rolling around laughing, nearly striking the sides of the tube. She flew along silently for a little while, enjoying the rush of air and the effortless flying. She started to daydream about fields and rivers and seeing them from very high up. After a time, Andrew nudged her.

"It's time," Andrew said.

"For what?" asked Lucy, startled out of her dream.

"The guy ahead of me told me that we're almost there. He can see the detector from here. Oh, Lucy, look! It's antimatter! Here they come!"

Lucy strained to look, and saw a proton that looked exactly like her; only it had an opposite charge. It was like looking into a mirror, raising your left hand, and having the mirror raise its right hand back at you. Lucy had never been so amazed. She knew that antimatter was supposedly dangerous as that's what her grandfather had told her. But this "Lucy antimatter" was flying along happily just as she was. Perhaps it had even been singing earlier, and had been told to shut up by a mean antiproton that looked exactly like that mean proton. Her thoughts of a whole parallel universe made her head spin. She looked over at Andrew for some kind of support.

"Hey Lucy!" shouted Andrew. "Isn't that amazing? Look, there's an antiproton that looks just like me! It even has my quarks, and ... oh, Lucy, We're about to..." Lucy and Andrew braced themselves.

BAMHH!

Lucy watched as Andrew broke apart and turned into a shower of other particles. She saw that he had made a really good charm-anticharm quark pair, and quite a few leptons and mesons. They disappeared so quickly she couldn't quite be sure ... She had done the same thing, burst apart, but she was unsure as to the kinds of particles she had made. At first there was a feeling of being huge. Then she felt like two bottom quarks, maybe a W particle pair. Being a neutrino was fun for a second as well, being completely neutral was a new thing for Lucy, She realized that the physicists would not be able to detect her and she giggled. She soon decayed again, though. She was a fast jet of particles. Andrew's voice came from somewhere behind her.

"Hey Lucy! Did you see my charm-anticharm quark pair?" He spun around happily.

"Yes, said Lucy. "You were wonderful! But there's one thing that's bothering me," Lucy frowned.

"What's that?" asked Andrew.

"I don't know what I was. Did you see what kind of particles I made? Did I make a top quark?"

"I don't know," said Andrew. "What were you after we all collided?"

Lucy thought carefully. "Well, I think I was a W-anti W pair, and a bottom quark-antibottom quark pair. Then I felt a neutrino of some sort, I think an antimuon, and a muon, and there was an up and an antidown quark in there too. What would that make me?"

"Oh, Lucy, I think you were a top quark!!"

"I was? Oh yay for top quarks! Yay for me!" Lucy spun around and hugged Andrew. Lucy and Andrew, who were no longer protons but jets of particles, streamed happily away.

THE ANTHROPOMORPHIZED SUBATOMIC ZOO
BY KRISTINA KRAMER (1989)
BIOCHEMISTRY MAJOR

The year is 1931. The day is dawning over Poughkeepsie. They sleep below but the fire burns unremittingly. I am born in the blink of an eye on such a day from that very fire. I am born, and one million others like me are born every second per centimeter squared. I am omniscient, omnipotent, and omnipresent. I am a neutrino. I pass through matter unhindered. I remain undeterred by ineffectual gravitational, electromagnetic and so-called strong forces. I speak of myself; I speak of my brothers. I speak of the massive continuum of neutrinos that has existed since the dawn of the universe. We exist until the end. I predict that the fate of the cosmos is in our hands. We will carry the universe until the load becomes too great. And then...

You humans are rabid with ignorance. You know nothing of our power. Your science has overlooked us for centuries upon centuries. You, who speak with such pride of your education, your job, your possessions and your family. What do these things mean? You live for several decades and expire. You are useless. You are like so much unstable matter. You mean nothing in the schema of the universe. You refuse to see beyond what is readily available to your eye. We are hidden within the neutron within the atom that composes all matter, living or not. Matter that is very like that of your own, small sub-universe. But we are timeless and boundless. We exist endlessly in the continuum. You fail to imagine us flowing into and out of all that is a part of your world on every day that is yours. We, for our part, know nothing of the day. There is no force that affects our boundlessness of wisdom and triumph.

What? Can it be true? Can this day truly be like no other since the beginning of time? These humans have come close to discovering our secret. The one they call Wolfgang has seen the breakdown of our parent neutron. He knows that energy is conserved in the separation of brother proton and brother electron, yet he is puzzled by the strange angle they produce. He claims there is another of us, one that is invisible. I linger, observing, as usual. I . . . you must forgive me I . . . I'm not quite feeling myself today . . .I seem to be overcome by some force. How can this be happening? I'm changing. I feel th....

The year is 1956. I have absorbed my brother's thoughts and I continue them in earnest. He has not died. He has changed form. His usefulness was required elsewhere. We carry on in the endless spirit of the continuum.

You know we exist in our ghostly state. You hunger to find us. On this day your search is culminating. You have built an apparatus that you hope will work as well as the fire has worked at producing us. I pass through the skull of one of your physicists to get a better view of what is transpiring. Before my very eyes one million million enter the continuum every second per square centimeter. You have found our secret! Your "reactor material" decays and we experience massive births.

It is the end of your ignorance. You explain our ghostliness by calling us chargeless and massless. You (perhaps inadequately) dub the only force that controls our destinies "weak". You feel empowered. You find we come in generations, which differ surprisingly from one another. You watch us transform into brother electron, cousin muon, and cousin tau, aided by our gargantuan comrade, W Boson. Having solved this puzzle, you relax, secure in the knowledge of your superiority.

The year is 5 Billion A.D. I have been here, waiting for you. I am the neutrino. I am all-powerful. Your foresight never predicted what is to happen on this day. You called us massless. If only you had revered us, in our perfection, you would never have dismissed us following your initial postulates. You never considered our mass and how much of the universe is carried by us. Today you learn. The time has come. Our continuum draws closer and closer. We draw together along with cousin baryons. Your "expanding universe" is gone. We are omnipotent ... We are omniscient . . . We are omnipres-

CRUNCH.

A SUBATOMIC LOVE STORY
BY NANA KORANTSEN HAGAN (2002)
BIOCHEMISTRY MAJOR

I'm Elly and I'm an electron. Over one hundred years ago, amidst glowing glass tubes and a hum of electricity, I was born. My birth was celebrated all over the world. There were balls in England, fetes in France, and a Nobel banquet in Sweden, all in honor of me. Fame came easily to me but love lingered. As I grew older, I developed properties such as charge and spin, and that's when I caught the attention of another particle. His name was Peter Nucleon and he was a proton. Peter was discovered after I was and is thus a bit younger than I am, but age doesn't matter. What mattered then was that we were both attracted to each other. Since I was negatively charged and Peter was positively charged, I was convinced that we were a perfect match. Unfortunately romance, like science is never that simple. Within the next few paragraphs I will tell you about my short-lived relationship with Peter, and how he left me for another particle.

Peter and I grew up in the same town. We were both a little shy but I knew he was attracted to me just as I was to him. With time, our situation got better and we began to date. Peter tried very hard to keep our relationship a secret but I loved my proton nonetheless. Anytime I saw Peter I was hurled into a state of frenzy. Peter was like the sun to me and I revolved around him like a heavenly body. Unfortunately we were not destined to be. According to the books of physics and love, opposites attract and love is supposed to conquer all, but how do I explain the heart-wrenching events of the early 1930s?

There had been reports in our town that Peter was seeing someone else. I did not want to "quantum jump" to conclusions, and I did not want to approach Peter to ask him about these rumors. Instead I asked my friends for evidence. Mr. Rutherford told me that he had once caught sight of Peter at a local restaurant. He said Peter sat at a table for two. Even though there was no one in the second seat at the time,

Mr. Rutherford was convinced that the seat was taken because there was a plate of food there. Mr. Rutherford then told me that his initial thought was that the second plate of food was mine, but on inspection realized that the food on it was just like the food on Peter's plate. Mr. Rutherford was well aware that my appetite was nowhere as big as Peter's so whomever Peter was with must have been as big as he was. Unfortunately Mr. Rutherford was in a hurry so he could not stay long to find out who Peter's secret lover was.

Another friend, Mr. Chadwick, also told me about his observations. According to Mr. Chadwick, he had sent his niece Alphi over to Peter's house to get some salt for their evening meal. Apparently Peter was not home at the time. Alphi however met another particle in Peter's house. Peter would certainly have given Alphi the salt, as Peter is kind and positive by nature. The particle Alphi met in Peter's house however was not like that at all. When Alphi asked for salt she neither said yes nor no. She was quite unresponsive.

Putting the information I received from Mr. Rutherford and Mr. Chadwick together, it became quite obvious that Peter was not only seeing, but also living with another particle. I was crushed. I had been led along all these years thinking that Peter and I were meant to be together forever. I had to go into counseling for a while to get over my depression. With time I came to understand why Peter had left me for the other particle (who I later found out was a neutron called Nora). The fundamental laws of physics seemed to predict this. Nora seemed to have a lot more in common with Peter than I did. First and foremost, Peter and Nora are approximately the same size so they did not look awkward together. Whenever I went out with Peter, strangers used to pass comments about how young and tiny I was and how big he was. One daring bar tender even refused to serve me alcoholic beverages and reprimanded Peter for taking me to a bar at such a late hour. Things like that must have made Peter feel uncomfortable and may also have been the reason why he wanted our relationship to remain a secret.

Another thing that Nora and Peter had in common was a strong force. I believed Peter and myself shared something special but according to Peter all we had was an electromagnetic force and nothing more. I was well aware of the fact that we shared an electromagnetic force but I guess we both had different opinions of what this force was. I thought the electromagnetic force that we shared was an all conquering and all binding force between us but Peter did not see it that way. He told me that the force he shared with Nora was the strongest force of all forces thus over riding the electromagnetic force that I shared with him.

A lot has happened since Peter left me for Nora. I no longer feel bitterness towards them. Peter and Nora are married now, and Mr. and Mrs. Nucleon live together in the center of the atom. They have six lovely quarks all together. Peter had told me that someday he wanted to have quarks of his own and he also hoped that whoever he settled down with would also be able to have quarks. I never told him that I was barren and thus could not have quarks of my own. I guess in the long run it did not matter anyway.

It has been one hundred years since my discovery and I remain single. Because of my experience with Peter, I have become very picky about dating, as I do not think I can stand another heartbreak. I am in search of a particle that is approximately the same size as I am. I like to spin during my spare time and my partner should enjoy spinning too. I am quite stable and search for the same stability in my partner. I do not want lifetime to be a limiting factor in our relationship. My ideal particle should also be able to feel the electromagnetic force as I do and last but certainly not least the particle should be positively charged. I still believe that opposites attract. There has been talk of a new particle in my town. I have not met him yet but I've been told that he's a positron and fulfils most of my requirements. I look forward to meeting him, and hope that he does not mind the age difference.

Stories

JURASSIC QUARK
BY JODY WEBB (1997)
COGNITIVE SCIENCE MAJOR

"I knew this would happen," grumbled the middle-aged man, as the Town Car lumbered into the gas station lot.

"It was unavoidable, given the equipment demands and flight costs," quipped the driver. It had been a long night, and the passenger was in no mood to argue. "Just gas this puppy and get us to the airstrip."

"Yes, Mr. Lepton," replied the driver.

"Oh, and Mann, get me some doughnuts."

Mann began filling the fat, gas-guzzling car. "I tried to explain to him that he would run over budget, but he wouldn't hear it. After financing the Accelerator and the jet, well, we just didn't have the cash to hire personnel. We tried to talk some former Soviet scientists into helping, but they all had excuses, like selling nuclear weapons to the highest bidder or something. Ha! They'll be sorry they missed out on this one!"

The pump cut out, signaling a full tank. Mann replaced the nozzle and headed into the Quicky Mart store. "Unless we get someone dumb enough to handle the radioactive detecto-meter, I don't think I'll be able to manage the quark containment all by my self..." Mann stopped short of completing his thought. There, standing behind the sales counter, was the answer.

"That'll be $21.93, mister. Anything else?" The clerk was wearing a crisp blue work shirt, not unlike the kind one would expect a gas station clerk to be wearing. A patch sewn above the left breast pocket boldly proclaimed; Welcome to Quicky Mart my name is Bob.

The jet was soon airborne, en route to the secret island. "So, you see Bob, I, Mr. Lepton, am a businessman and a visionary. I had formerly been working in high energy physics, but as you may know, most people do not find science all that, *entertaining*"

"Duh, yea, I know what yuh mean, mister Lepton. I hated high school."

"Of course, Bob. Now, while most physicists were simply seeing particle trace diagrams, I was seeing an opportunity. When I told them my idea, they said it couldn't be done. Said I was crazy. But with my money and the sheer technical skill of Mr. Candy Mann, it is now a reality."

The middle-aged man leaned closer to Bob and, with bated breath, whispered, "Son, I have created a Subatomic Zoo."

Bob seemed unfazed by the news. "So's, why do yuh need me?"

"Well Bob, we ran over budget, and cuts had to made somewhere. We decided to cut down on the quality of personnel."

"Heh, you're a pretty smart guy Mr. Lepton."

Having landed smoothly, the jet taxied down the runway and parked near a small hangar. The three occupants deplaned, walked across the tarmac, and hopped into a Jeep.

"Uh, why do they call you Candy Mann?" queried Bob, as the Jeep trundled along the jungle road.

"Mr. Mann is a genius," replied Lepton. "And his mastery of Quark Flavor is matched only by his oneness with the Weak side of the Force."

"Er, I thought there was a dark side of the force," began Bob. Lepton quickly cut him off, "That was long, long ago, in a galaxy far, far away, Bob."

Now the control complex was in sight. Mann pulled the Jeep up to the front door and engaged the parking brake. Lepton explained to Bob that he would be monitoring some equipment. "No worries, Bob, this is as easy as ringing up a 16 ounce coke and a chilidog. You'll be going down in history."

Mann had designed and, with Lepton's money, created all the subatomic attractions in the zoo. However, Lepton would not reveal the zoo to the general public until the main attraction had been created: a free top quark! The universe had not seen the likes of the top quark since prehistoric times. Today they planned to create one.

"OK. Bob, what we need you to do is sit here and watch these meters." Lepton directed Bob over to a monitor console. "When I ask you to, watch these lights and tell us immediately if they turn red. Never take you're eyes off them. They can change from green to red and back again very quickly and if you aren't watching, you'll miss it."

Mann had missed a critical design flaw when designing this console, and, consequently, it leaked some sort of curious radiation, intense at its source but dissipating within a meter. Not having an engineer on hand to fix the problem, Mann let it go, convinced he could con some schmoe into watching the console. He was right.

Mann and Lepton had planned carefully for the free top quark. They created a custom drift chamber to monitor its movement, as well as a massless, positively charged containment fence to keep it locked within the attraction limits.

Now everything was set. Mann sat down at the Accelerator controls.

"3000 GeV and climbing!" he exclaimed.

"6000 GeV!"

"8000!"

"Keep it up!" shouted Lepton, wringing his hands in obvious anticipation and agony.

"10,000 GeV!!" A groaning sound could now be heard emanating from the depths of the building.

"Bob, are the lights all green?" Mann yelled.

"Uh, yea."

"Punch it!" Lepton howled in a frenzy. "This better work!"

Mann pressed a button. A sharp nurrrrrrr sound rang through the air.

And then all was silent.

"Houston, we have a top quark," Mann exclaimed. Lepton was bouncing off the walls.

Mann walked over to an electrical panel and began making a few adjustments, while Bob, utterly missing the import of the moment, fixed himself a cup of coffee and sat down at a random control console to contemplate the state of the oil in his pickup truck. He had just noticed that his left boot was untied and reached to tie it when Mann barked, "Bob, watch those meters!"

Setting the coffee down so that he could reach his boot, Bob searched the console for steady green lights, but found only buttons, knobs, and dials. A large plate over the controls read "Containment Fence Console." Tying his boot, he glanced around the room to find the original console to which Lepton had directed him. "Aha," he uttered, spying the panel across the room. Little did he recognize that, while he wasn't watching what he was doing, he had accidentally tied his left bootlaces onto his right boot.

"It's alive, it's alive," Lepton chanted. "Those arrogant pencil pushers at Fermilab can kiss my..." He never got to finish his sentence. Just as Bob rose to walk over to the console, he tripped on his boots and came crashing to the floor, and, in a futile effort to break his fall, flailed his arms madly, thwapping the coffee cup contents all over the control panel. Snap-crackle-pop.

"Argh! The containment fence is down!" Mann bellowed.

Lepton and Mann, though hoping the need would never arise, had prepared for the escape of a free quark. Lepton raced to a phone and punched in a number. A few seconds later, he slammed down the receiver.

"He's on his way. Let's get outta here."

The trio exited the control complex with great haste. Twenty minutes later, a helicopter touched down outside the complex. A large, imposing individual jumped out, and the 'copter lifted off and disappeared into the sky.

"Gentlemen, I hear that we have a free quark," said the man, hefting a large black case.

"That's not the worst of it," Mann stammered. "It's the Top!"

Barry On is a member of the Eightfold Way, a secretive society of ninjas. A no-nonsense troubleshooter for hire, rumor has it that Barry has developed an invincible technique for just this occasion: the antitop Fist!

"I'm gonna need a little intelligence briefing on this Top quark, Mann," demanded On. "So ya better be straight and no lies. How big is this sucker?"

"It's almost 200 GeV's."

"Damn, that's big. What do ya feed that thing?"

"Anything it wants, but usually..."

"Ah, doesn't matter," On replied, "dead or alive, either way, I can do the job. Course, dead's a lot easier." He reached into the case and produced a wicked looking gun of some sort. "This .44 caliber gluon cannon can drop a charging quark at 50 nanometers. If it can die, this will kill it."

"And if it can't," Lepton mused, an eyebrow raised in interest.

"It'll be in so much pain, it'll wish that it could."

Just then a loud snapping sound alerted the group as to the whereabouts of the Top. "It's eating the Accelerator!" Mann shouted.

On raced up the hill that surrounded the complex and scanned the island. Sure enough, the big, ugly Top had burrowed into the ground and was rending and tearing at the Accelerator pipeline. "Eat this!" cried On, squeezing off a shot at the Top.

The monstrous Top turned its destructive attention toward On, while Lepton raced up the stairs of an observation deck to watch the battle. At least Mann and Bob had the sense to get the hell out of there.

"Now I gotcha." On carefully aimed his piece at the charging Top.

BANG

"Uh oh," On muttered as the gluon sliced thin air where the Top had been. It was quicker than it looked. It could move at speeds near c, after all.

"Ahhh!" On sought cover behind a palm tree and was nearly behind it when the Top collided mightily with the tree trunk. The collision stopped Top in its tracks, but not without energy conservation, mind you: the tree was blown to smithereens and On flew like a doll through the air, landing quite a ways from the gluon cannon.

"Oh no!" Lepton was sticking out like a sore thumb all alone up there on the observation deck, and Top turned its wrath on him.

"Get back you monster," Lepton warned, grabbing a fire ax from the platform. Ten meters below him, the Accelerator pipeline lay exposed and active, generating massive particle collisions.

Top feinted high then struck low, but miraculously, Lepton parried and riposted with a vicious overhead smash. "I knew all that fencing at Vassar would pay off!"

Lepton's luck ran out, though, and the creation got the upper hand over the creator. Bearing down with its massive 200 GeV weight, it forced Lepton up and over the observation deck railing.

"Noooooooo...." gasped Lepton as he fell to a swift demise in the bowels of the Accelerator, pulverized by positron collisions.

Suddenly, a war cry from behind!

"Die!" On shrieked. Assuming his trademark Quark defense stance, he unleashed the devastating antitop Fist, annihilating the Top in furious clash of energy!

ATOMIC LOVE
BY ELIZABETH HAWLEY (1993)
ENGLISH MAJOR

One wintry evening, Eric the Electron was settled in front of the fireplace reading his favorite book. Shortly later his wife, Priscilla the Proton, joined him. As the two sat, laughing and reminiscing, each of their three children quietly crept up to sit with them.

"Mommy, Daddy," said the baby particle, "Tell us how you guys met."

"Yes, yes!" Exclaimed Photon, the eldest son, "Just when did you fall in love?"

After several minutes of urging, the blushing, yet pleased, parents finally caved in.

"Well," began Eric the Electron, "It all began in a rather, shall we say, unconventional way..."

"We met on a game show!" piped up Priscilla the Proton. "The Love Connection!" She then proceeded to tell them the story.

"Good afternoon, ladies and gentlemen, I am pleased you could all join us for today's show. I'm your host, John the Positron. Now, let's meet our three male contestants."

John gestures grandly with his left arm, as the backdrop behind him slowly lifts to reveal two nervous men, anxiously straightening their ties and tugging at their socks, seated on either side of an empty chair.

"Contestant number one!" John the Positron directs his attention to the cue card in his right hand, while he points to a skinny guy in a cheap suit with his hair slicked back and parted in the middle. "Peter the Positive Pion! Peter says he works as an intermediary exchange particle between nucleons. His mass is one seventh of that of a proton, and he has a positive charge. Peter also wants to add that his sign is +. Well, Peter, how does it feel to be on the show?"

"Um, well, uh... I dunno (hee hee). I guess it's great, um, well..."

"Fabulous! Contestant number two is Quin the Top Quark!" It takes a moment for John to realize that he is pointing to an empty chair. "Oh, dear... well, it appears as though Mr. Top-Quark was not available in time for the taping of our show. As a matter of fact, our staff is still trying to get in touch with him. You see, nobody has ever really seen Mr. Top Quark. He was, however, kind enough to send statistical information and interests, so there is strong evidence of his existence."

"Quin says he works as a fundamental particle inside a black hole. He enjoys tennis and baseball. He has a charge of positive two-thirds, and a mass ranging anywhere from seventy-five to two hundred and fifty times that of a proton. Mr. Quark also says that he sometimes feels trapped, as though he were trying to escape from a glass bowl, but that the walls which hold him inside are infinitely high, and the more he struggles, the more the strong force exerts itself, and the more he realizes that he will never break free... hmm, well, isn't that, um, rather interesting. Perhaps, Mr. Top Quark is also an amateur poet, as well, hey? Hee, hee, well, let's move on."

"And finally, we have contestant number three, Eric the Electron!" Eric had finally calmed down his nerves to the point where he seemed much more stable than contestant number one. "Eric is also a fundamental particle, and he makes up one of the three parts of the atom. He has a charge of negative one, and a small mass. Oh, that's very interesting! Eric, how does it feel to be so light?"

"It feels great, John! Like a weight off my shoulders!" Eric replied.

"Hmm, yes, I'd imagine. Well, let's meet our female contestant, since she will be choosing between these charming men." The stage's left wall suddenly swings around, so that a woman seated in a plush, red chair is now exposed to the audience.

"Meet Priscilla the Proton! Priscilla works inside the atom, as a matter of fact; she holds the esteemed position of hydrogen nucleus. She has a charge of positive one and a mass of one. Priscilla, let's start the questioning with you."

"Ok," she replied gently, batting her eyelashes and swiveling in her chair.

"What do you look for in a relationship?"

"Well," Priscilla appeared deep in thought, "I look for stability. I need to know that I can count on him if and whenever I need to. I am not interested in one of those here today, gone tomorrow relationships."

"And what sort of man do you find yourself attracted to?"

"Well, it's rather strange," Priscilla began, "but I seem drawn, as if by some electromagnetic force as inherent as gravity, towards certain men."

"Contestant number one, how would you respond to—uh, oh!" John the Positron glances at the chair where Peter the Positive Pion once sat. "Oh, well, I was afraid this might happen. Apparently Peter the Positive Pion has decayed. No, no, no! Ladies and gentlemen, don't be alarmed. You see, the average life span of a pion is only 10^{-8} seconds, as it is a rather unstable particle. Therefore, we took a risk by admitting him on the show. This is really rather amazing, though since the only other particle I know of with the ability to decay like this is the neutron when it undergoes radioactive beta decay, and subsequently breaks down into a proton an electron and a neutrino. Peter broke down into a positive muon and a neutrino. I suspect the weak force is responsible for all this. Well, it's a shame. We shall just have to carry on without him."

"But, Mr. Positron," Priscilla cried. "There is only one contestant left!"

"Oh? Hey! How about that! Well, due to unfortunate circumstances, you two will have to entertain the Love Connection Weekend package together. We'll pay expenses, of course. How does that sound, Priscilla?"

"Well, I guess it's all right, I mean, I didn't get to ask any questions or anything..."

"Great!" John cuts her off. "I'm so glad you agree! Let me tell you where the two of you will be vacationing.

Wow! You're going to spend three days and three nights inside a linear accelerator! Tell them all about it, Joan!"

"Yes, John, that's correct! We'll fly you and your date, all expenses paid, to the Stanford Linear Accelerator Center in California! There you will be injected through one end of the linac, and then through an electric field. But that's not all! When you emerge at the other end of the accelerator, you'll have higher energy, and be moving at the speed of light! Now how does that sound? Keep in mind that this is an extra-special, once in a lifetime trip for Priscilla, since a proton trip through a linear accelerator costs a lot of money and is a very complicated process. But here at the Love Connection, it is yours for absolutely no cost!"

"Hey, that sounds fabulous, John," Eric interrupted. "But I think Priscilla and I would rather just go out for dinner. We're from a conservative generation."

"Yes," Priscilla agreed, "Shall we go for Chinese?"

"So you see children," Eric concluded, "that is the story of how your mother and I met and eventually fell in love. I guess you could say it was the gravitational force – the force which acts on all particles with mass."

"No, honey! The electromagnetic force surely must be responsible! Don't you remember? Equal, yet opposite charges will be attracted to one another," Priscilla insisted.

"That's great!" Exclaimed Electron Jr., "Now tell us how we got here!"

"Bedtime!" Priscilla cried. "That story will be told at a later…ahem, much later date!"

Then everyone bade goodnight and went to bed.

MICKEY SPILANE UCHITEL IN THE SUBATOMIC ZOO
BY MICHAEL UCHITEL (1989)
PHILOSOPHY MAJOR

The name's Mickey, Mickey Spilane Uchitel. I'm a private D. I work in the subatomic zoo and believe me baby it ain't no picnic. Oh yeah, most of the time, everybody follows the rules, but now and again some particle steps over the line. The atomic police do no good. Well, you know, about the only thing the cops are good at is hanging around the Dunkin' Donuts exchanging stories of their accelerated days and winking at the ions. The year is 1961. It was a cool day. All of a sudden, this beautiful particle walks into my office and plops down on a chair. I offer her an electromagnetic charge but she just starts right into her story. She was desperately looking for a dude named Eta who she had never seen but who she had deduced must be running around with the Meson gang.

Yeah, I knew the Mesons; they were one of the Hadron groups that had been spotted running around since the early 50's. Unlike the Baryons (the other faction of the Hadrons) there were only seven known members of Mesons, all with strangeness from one to negative one, I might add. Yeah, these were the Pion and Kaon brothers. These particles were bad with charges ranging from negative one to positive one. These particles took on a hexagonal shape when charted on police records with that neutral pion sitting right in the middle. He was definitely the gang leader. These boys were quick, not as quick as the Baryons, but they were gone anywhere from 10^{-8} to 10^{-16} seconds, so they were tough to catch. Their masses were between 1/7 and 1/2 of the mass of that bad boy, Mr. Proton. But that's not what bothered me. She was right – the middle dude of the baryons, the Sigma Zero, had his right hand man, the Lambda, right in the middle with him. Since these Hadron groups both appeared hexagonal on police charts (obviously suggesting they like to organize in much the same ways) she figured that the bad old neutral pion must have his own right hand man with that same old zero charge and zero strangeness.

This dame had her head on straight. Now, she also tells me that I can bet my bottle of cheap whiskey that this Eta dude also had half the mass of Mr. Proton. That's a bet I would gladly have made. Boy was she on the ball, but she didn't have to tell this stooge that Eta was probably going around with no spin at all. She had basically done my work for me – she'd practically identified the eighth member of the Meson gang and seemed to have filled out the Hadrons as a whole. I figured that all that was left for me to do was to head down to the nearest bubble chamber bar and grill (with the pool hall in the back) and wait for this Eta guy to mosey on through. I told her I got six joules of energy a day plus whatever expenditures I might incur. She agreed and so it happened on that cool night in '61. I spotted Pion Zero's right hand man and was able to add him to the predicted place on the Meson police chart. Well, I have to go now. Me and the dame who was looking for Eta have a date to get together in Billi's accelerator and pool hall. Don't take any wooden gluons!

THE NEUTRON STORY: A TALE OF CHARGE AND DECAY
BY CHRIS PERRY (1998)
PHILOSOPHY MAJOR

Neutron was in the kitchen boiling a full pot of gamma photons for dinner. As the pot neared boiling, more and more quick flashes played about the room. No other lights were on as the sun set outside. Neutron could hear Electron watching football in the living room, sitting in his favorite chair, the one closest to the television. He almost always sat in that one chair. Sometimes he'd sit at the very end of the couch, or even hover near the door, excited like a dog that has to go. But as dinner was almost ready, he was in his same old place.

Neutron served the meal. They sat in silence eating, spinning a little, uncomfortably. There was no love in their marriage. They'd found each other in a lonely corner of a bubble chamber–just happened to be in the same place at the same time. Off like a shotgun to the chapel from there. It wasn't till they hit the wedding bed that they realized there was no real attraction between them. Years later, they'd pass close in the house, maybe even recoil gently from each other. Electron would go out every day to work on the power lines while Neutron stayed home, restless, aching on the inside.

Electron threw down his spoon. "These photons are cold, woman! I come home from a long day running up and down the power lines, and I don't even get a dinner at the right energy for me to swallow. Do you hate me that much? Do you like watching me wallow in the ground here?" he vibrated. "I do the best I can, Lec. I'm sorry."

"I'm going bowling with the guys. I can grab something on the way. Just hope, for your sake, that throwing myself against some photomultiplier tubes for a couple of hours wears me out or else." He stormed out of the room, leaving Neutron staring at the gradually dimming flashes, then out the window into the face of a colder, darker entropy.

Later in the night, Neutron lay in bed dozing off. Three in the morning and he wasn't home yet. Neutron dreamed only of change, felt something welling up inside. How long would it be before it broke out, before it, anything, happened? The light grew dimmer as Neutron slipped into unconsciousness.

Neutron began to dream, alone there in bed. "Where am I?" Neutron walked down the hallway, slowly spinning this way and that. There were doors along each wall, and Neutron felt as if each door would give some sort of vision, something horrible or something grand. She opened one door and was immediately grabbed and pulled in. Laughter and then the lights came on. Surrounding her, darting this way and that, taunting with collision, were dozens of large, strange creatures. Neutron shivered, frightened. Then one of the strange creatures went up to her and said, "I have been sent by Cosmic Ray. Ray has seen your plight and so ordered me to reveal myself to you, for when the time is right you too will decay!" At that instant the strange creature horribly melted away.

Out one way from its body shot an electron. "Oh my god. Electron! What are you doing here? Help me Lec" But he was gone in an instant through a small portal in one of the walls of the room. She turned back to where the creature had been. There was still something there. Looking closer, she realized it was two things running around each other, changing and shifting in weird psychedelic displays that made them hard to look at for too long. They approached, oscillating strangely before her. "We are neutrinos. Look at us. We are hideous, without charge, unable to keep a single form for too long. Can you see us?"

"Yes, barely. But... but I shouldn't. I've heard of you and," she stopped cold. "Oh my god! That's not possible. Oh, the humanity! You have mass!" And the laughter returned, now with a double voice sounding like a sort of chilling trilling echo in her head. "You too will decay, dear Neutron." And she woke up, shivering, screaming.

"Neutron, Neutron, wake up. You're having a bad nightmare." It was Electron, hot and sweaty, just back from bowling. "Oh, Lec, it was horrible! There were these giant muons standing around me and one of them melted and you came flying out and then instead of you and the muon there was these two neutrinos, awful horrible. They were a muon neutrino and an electron antineutrino. Both. And, oh god, Lec, they had mass! I could see them." She shook uncontrollably.

"Shhhh. Quiet now, Neutron. I'm here for you. It was just a bad dream. There is nothing to worry about. Everything will be fine. Just…"

"Ohhh. Lec, I feel so funny. I feel like something's happening inside me. It's not bad but, oh, it hurts. Lec, what's happening to me? What's happened to us, to our marriage?"

"I'm calling the hospital, Neut. Just hold on and they'll send an ambulance right over. Don't worry. Everything's gonna be okay." He dialed 911 as Neutron lay in their bed, shivering in the dark.

"How's my wife, doc? What's wrong with her?" The neutral pions were running around the room, checking monitors, and turning knobs. Doctor K looked solemn. "Well, Mr. Particle, it's hard to say. She could just be excited, but we won't know until we can get a closer look. Now, I'm warning you, there's a chance it could be one of her quarks, in which case not even a transplant can do anything. We'll just have to wait and see." Just then, one of the pions came running up.

"Doctor K, Doctor K, I think that we're losing her! Hurry."

"Quick, get her into the chamber, stat. Mr. Particle, you might not want to watch this. This is a very dangerous, still experimental, procedure. It might go badly."

"I understand, Doc. Do anything you have to, but please just save my wife." They loaded Neutron into 'the chamber' and sealed the door behind her. "Everything will be okay Neut. Just hold on."

Dr. K turned on the machine. On the scope he could see Neutron's quarks, but no neutron. "Well, her colors and strangeness seem to check out, but, wait a second. Nurse, is this thing working right?"

"All systems check out, Dr. K."

"That's Dr. Kaon to you, miss! But, look at this. Mr. Particle, one of your wife's down quarks seems to be unstable. This quark, this thing inside her, is vibrating in a different mode. It desperately seems to want to change."

"What'll that do to her? Will she live?"

"It's too early to tell."

Just then there was a shriek from the chamber. Everyone in the room turned. Dr. K shuddered. There, on the screen, Neutron's weak down quark suddenly became an up quark. There was another scream. "Quick, nurse, get her out of 'the chamber'!"

The door to 'the chamber' swung open with a hiss and a gush of steam. When it cleared, Dr. K, Electron and the pion nurses were crowded around to see what had become of poor Neutron. Another pion fainted. Doctor Kaon gasped. But Electron smiled. Neutron had become Proton, attracting at last her husband. And beside her lay a negative W boson, "Quick," said Doctor K, "Get her out of there. That negative W boson might decay at any moment."

Electron grabbed Proton and they embraced, running around each other. Just then, the boson decayed. All turned away, and when they looked back, there was a brand new little Electron, resting quietly in his ground state. "Look, Lec, now we have a son."

"Yes, darling. Let's go home and make the nuclear family we've always dreamed of in the suburbs with four forces and stability. Cheer up Doctor K! Thanks to you our marriage is saved, Neutron is Proton and is okay, and we have a little baby Electron junior of our very own."

"Yes, but there's something you should know. According to my readings of the birth, you have another child. One that's hideous and deformed."

"What! Where is it? Where's my other baby?" cried Proton.

"He... it is long gone now, Proton." Doctor K turned away. "Somewhere out there, is your electron's nemesis. He'll be back, don't worry, but who can say what havoc this unruly little electron antineutrino will wreak upon the world." They were all silent then, vibrating with contemplation of the evil yet to come.

QUARKS, A HOT PARTICLE STORY
BY DARMY E. MOTA (1998)
COMPUTER SCIENCE MAJOR

"Whee! Yippee! Let's do it again," said Red, the little quark, to his big brother, Green, as they finished their cosmic race.

"Yeah, that was fun, but this time, let's call our cousins too." They told their gluon friends to bring a couple of friends, who were scattered somewhere else across the incredibly hot fireball they lived in.

Red and Green were from the Up family, and they had a lot of cousins and gluon friends. Their cousins where all from the Up family, and the Bottoms, the Tops, the Downs, the Charms and the Stranges too. Their names, coincidentally, were Blue, Green and Red. There were in fact huge groups belonging to these families, all having the same names, and their favorite hobby was to race freely in the plasma-like environment they lived in. They were all born nanoseconds ago, maybe even less than a nanosecond ago, when their creator, Spot, threw them in all directions. Spot was tired of being so full of "stuff". He weighed a lot, and there was a lot of pressure on his body of inert particles. He finally decided that he was hot and tired, and vanished as all the happy quarks came cheering out of his exploding body.

"I'm feeling tired, Red," yelled Green to his quark brother. "Are the gluons back with our other cousins? They should be by now!" he continued. "Yeah, I know, let's play without them then," said Green as he quickly rushed back from some place that to us would seem like 100 miles away. Green was an expert runner and that is why Red always looked up to him. He wanted to be able to get faster and faster, like his brother; he was going so fast that light could not accurately show his location. This is an easy thing for quarks, and they were always racing. Whoosh! Whoosh! "Let's go Faster!" That is all in the life of the quarks, including our fellows Red and Green.

"I wonder why all the gluons that we sent to get the other quarks never came back." Green was a little worried.

He knew that his friends the gluons should be able to find other quark families and then, like magic, pull them towards the sender. This is the way that gluons were meant to be, telling other quarks where their quark cousins are and pulling them to meet them at some other place. But it seemed to Green that maybe the gluons were not strong enough. Who, he thought, could go after a free running quark and catch up to it? No, sir, there is no way that the gluons could really do what they were supposed to, because we are way too fast for them so they have almost no control over us.

"Maybe our gluon friends can't reach us because we are too fast," said Green. "I guess we'll have to see if we can find a couple quarks to hang out with and then decide what to do. I am starting to get bored with just running around. And man, this place is hot!" Green was right, there was nothing else the wimpy gluons could do. In fact, they could only go 10^{-15} meters without stopping, and these quarks loved racing way beyond those small distances. They had no limit on where to go because they were free and full of new energy. Not even the mighty gluons would be able to stop their constant racing.

Green and Red loved to race, but they had a major quest in mind. They had to find their sister, Blue, who had been lost since they were all created in the very first fraction of a nanosecond, when Spot gave them freedom. Now, it was up to them to find the millions... billions of cousins, and ask about their little sister. Red was very fond of his sister, and he wanted to teach her how to run as fast as Green.

"I can't wait to see my little sister. I need to share all these things you have taught me about my other cousins. She will be really excited!" said Red to his big brother after searching a couple of millimeters for her.

Green warned his brother. "You should rest a little bit, I think you are getting too excited now, and that could be bad for you. Remember what happened to those guys who were too anxious to reach the speed of light?"

Red looked a little worried, and tried to remember the story that Green told him a while before. "Yes, you can get tired and then, just then, nobody knows why exactly, but they will come after you! The same gluons that we have learned to use for fun, will come after you and pull you, and then you might end up hitting a cousin quark, and he'll fall down and get pulled back by the other evil gluons, and–" his brother had said. Green had stopped, because he could not continue saying what he himself could not understand. He certainly did not know what might happen next, but he was indeed scared of the possibilities. And Green should not worry. Others worried with stories that are shrouded in mystery.

Green changed the subject. "Hey, little Red, look, it's another group of quarks, maybe..." And so they rushed into that group of particles to see if they knew anyone.

"Nope, the Blue you are looking for is not here, maybe she got lost in another one of those new big groups I've seen," said one of the other quarks. Red saw a gluon friend pacing back and forth between that quark and another little Red quark.

"Hey, who is your little gluon fellow?" Green asked.

"Oh, him? He's just Glenn, he's been my friend since I got a little tired, and he stays close to me now. He tells me all that goes on with my red sister. Nothing bad with this gluon so far, I think I like him."

But Green almost dropped his jaw when he heard that. He was not happy that someone was telling such a lie in front of his little brother, Red. "Gluons can be deceiving," Green said to himself.

"What, you like your gluon friend?" Green asked perplexed.

But the other quark answered, "Anything wrong, pal? Gluons bring us closer together, I think. Look, there comes Glenn, again. Hold on."

Red and Green's friend greeted Glenn, exchanged a couple thoughts about the heat, and said goodbye to him. "See, my friend? They are harmless, even my little sister plays with Glenn the gluon and some other gluons. Since they have been around, we have come closer to other quarks. See over there, next to her? That is Cyan, our strange little Blue quark. Gluons bring us new friends from time to time, and she came a short time ago. We are a little community around here."

Red was excited about meeting new friends, and this could be the perfect opportunity to ask even more people about his sister. Green did not feel the same way, though, so he stepped aside and took Red with him for a moment.

"We have got to talk. I think that these guys are not feeling well. Just look at them! They are not feeling like racing anymore and they look more tired. I would sure miss going fast and running past everyone else. I'm always a winner, but I never do any extreme things. These down quarks are playing with their gluons...Oh, Lord! I can see lots of other quark families around there. And they are coming together! We are going to be squeezed by all these people!"

But Green was wrong, and a group of mighty gluons came along and kept the dozen or so quarks away from the group Green and Red were in. Red commented, "See, they are protecting us, I like these guys!"

"Sure, I guess we can let them get nearby. They are not so bad as I thought they were," said Green, with a bit of disappointment in his voice.

Soon, the quarks started forming more groups around them and the gluons were regulating the ways they were getting together. "No more than three quarks here, please. Move on to the next free group. Urn, we could use a Green quark here. Who wants to come along?" a tall gluon said boldly.

The gluons were monopolizing the growing universe with their Strong pull on the weakening quarks.

"I don't feel as fast anymore, Red, something is happening here!" Green tried to run past other moving groups of quarks, but then someone noticed and sent several gluons after him. And not even the speedy Green quark could break from their attraction, because they were too many gluons giving him little pulls and pushes. So he told red "No, I see that we can't make it because they have grown too strong with their Strong force. And it is getting really cold around here, I feel weak, Red. Maybe we can't do anything against them!"

Red saw that not even his older brother could escape from the hands of the gluons and he felt sad. In a moment, he was put together with another quark named Blue, and Green was in there too.

"Alright, you three are to be together," said the gluons. "You are going to form a bigger particle because we think that your colors look better when you are in groups, so stay there." And they tried to find a way to escape, but the harder they tried, the stronger their attraction was. They could not stay away from one another!

"Stay there! You make up a pretty proton, my friends," said one gluon.

And the gluons formed all kinds of particles out of the quarks. What we know today as neutrons, sigmas, lambdas, cascades and many other particles could now exist together. And with the new bigger particles, there came other helpers for the gluon's cause. There were photons, gravitons and W's and Z's, which were assigned to keep particles together with the others. That happened very quickly and then, all the smaller new particles started combining. They had no choice. All these photons, gluons, W's, Z's and gravitons contributed to forces known as electromagnetism, gravity, the strong force, and the weak force.

With all these force carriers doing their new job, slowly, the universe as we know it came to exist. Maybe some day the Strong pull between all the quarks and the bigger communities of particles will bring everything crashing into a small Spot, and then, just then perhaps, Red and Green will meet with their young lively sister and tell her about the lives that they have had.

But even now, every once in a while, Green and Red will get exited and try to recreate the energy they once had. They are confident that some day other quarks will break the bonds between them and fight for their freedom. If we ever do see a free quark, it will surely be Red or Green struggling their way across other atoms in search for their blue sister. And then, our human scientists determine out how they broke free as they go and cheer up the subatomic world again.

Stories

TRANSFORMATIONS
BY ELIZABETH FOOTE (1998)
ENGLISH MAJOR

"What are we going to be doing exactly?" asked Penelope, her positively charged form shivering in anticipation near her friend Patrick.

She didn't know exactly what was going on. One minute she'd been minding her own business, carrying on daily life with her own little electron spinning crazily around her, and the next minute they'd been ripped apart. And now here she was, trapped in a dark, vast chamber of some sort surrounded by protons like herself. Patrick had been in a hydrogen atom too and they had been friends forever. And now they'd both been unwillingly stripped of their fellow particles; Penelope felt somewhat naked.

"I don't know," Patrick replied agitatedly. "But I do know that I've never felt so much positive charge in one place! It's making me dizzy!"

Penelope was feeling a little disjointed, too. There was a confused, anxious hum in the air. She caught snippets of conversations:

"I hear it's a race!"

"What's the prize?"

"No, it's a transport vehicle! They're taking us to another world!"

"Oh, grow up. That kind of thing doesn't happen."

"It's the end, I tell you the end is coming!"

But no one seemed to know what was really happening. They were all as confused as Penelope. Penelope, still trying to adjust to her new free state, kept bumping into total strangers at random. "So sorry," she apologized continually at first, but soon it became evident that there was no point. It was so crowded that there was barely enough room to maneuver. Penelope tried to keep close to Patrick, clinging to some sense of familiarity.

"This is crazy!" she exclaimed. "Patrick, I'm scared. What's going to happen to us? I feel like we're on the verge of something disastrous."

"It'll be okay, Pen, I promise," he answered. "Just stick close by me, okay? We'll get through this."

"You think so?" came a voice next to them. They both turned to look, and were confronted with the face of another proton. "You think you'll make it out in one piece? Good luck. I wish you all the best." The proton was fairly aged, showing signs of wear. "But you have no idea what you're in for."

"What ever do you mean?" Penelope asked, fear tumbling around within the depths of her quarks.

"It's crazy in there," the old proton replied. "The first time I went through The Race, I thought it was the Judgment Day."

"The Race?" Penelope and Patrick said at the same time.

"I was just as young and stupid as you, and I didn't know what to expect. I was all fired up with anticipation. And then, they... well, they shot us into The Chamber."

"The Chamber?" Penelope repeated, becoming thoroughly terrified by the old proton's words. Patrick tried to swallow, but he was unsuccessful. The Chamber. The very name sounded ominous.

"Suddenly we were moving so fast we didn't know which end was up. We were all traveling faster than we'd ever gone before. And it was okay, sort of having fun even. Until we saw Them."

"Who?" Penelope whispered.

"The antiprotons."

Penelope and Patrick gasped. They'd heard of the antiprotons. They were that mythical race of particles that were exactly like them, except that they had a negative charge, like an electron. But no one had ever seen one, not anyone that the two of them had ever known.

"I watch as the antiprotons smash into my friends, their quarks flying everywhere beyond all recognition. They're transformed into new, strange, hideous particles that decay within an instant, and then they're gone." The old proton's face was lined with the pain at this memory. "And every time, I wait for my turn."

"But why?" Patrick choked, as he and Penelope had been moved to tears. "Why is this happening?"

"I think," the old proton said solemnly, "we're being punished. This is some sort of purgatory. Our punishment for every sin we committed in our lives is to be put through The Chamber and to wonder, every time, if we'll be the next to go. We watch our friends and our families get destroyed, always knowing that one day, we'll be next to be annihilated. I almost wish my time would come." The proton's voice grew tearful, and Patrick and Penelope huddled together in fear.

"What are you telling these children, Preston?" another voice shrilled from the darkness. "Why are you frightening them so?" A younger proton stormed angrily over to the old proton and bumped him.

"I'm telling them the truth, the way it should be told, Patty," Preston snapped back at her. "They have a right to know!"

"Children, don't listen to him," Patty said to them, her voice gentle. "Believe me, you're going to a better place. This process is just called Transformation. This state you're in now, it's so lowly and mean in comparison to what you could be. You'll have the chance to shine, to be greater than you ever could dream of being! You have no idea of the possibilities that are contained within you! One of you could contain Beauty, or even the ultimate Truth. Don't listen to this old proton. He doesn't understand that this is just a gateway to a better place. The horrors of this world will pass away, and you will see the perfect peace that lies beyond."

"And you?" Preston thundered. "How would you know? None of us knows what awaits us.

"You must have faith, Preston. You must have faith."

Suddenly there was a loud rumbling of gears, and the strange sound of the energy being gathered.

"Get ready!" yelled Preston, but his words were lost in the sudden surge of energy that propelled them all forward at an incredible rate of speed. Penelope found herself whirling headlong into infinity, vague shapes rushing past her dizzily. In a panic her muddled consciousness searched for Patrick, but she couldn't see him anywhere. Then, she saw Them.

They rushed at her with a deafening roar, and before she could even think. They were upon them, interspersing and rushing past. Explosions blasted all around her as she saw with horror protons crashing into the antiprotons and the quarks that bound them scattering in every direction. But the quarks weren't just scattering; they were binding together to form new particles, different from any proton that Penelope had ever seen. To Penelope, this explosive race of bombardments seemed to stand still as she watched particle after particle smash into each other, and new particles rise from the energy created. She floated, still, yet racing, transfixed by this cycle of death and rebirth.

All at once, she felt a jarring impact that knocked her from her reverie. In a blinding flash, before she could even think, she burst with an intense release of energy, her quarks splattering and recombining as she felt herself explode with the intensity of a thousand reactions. She felt herself grow suddenly massive in an ecstatic burst of activity, and she became Truth.

The moment of ecstasy stood still in time. Penelope didn't think; she just felt and understood. Then the feeling was gone and she could feel herself begin to come apart at the seams, decaying into smaller, lesser particles, shooting off jets of energy. As she dissolved, she attempted to mentally grasp onto the emotion, the incomprehensible mystery of what she had just experienced. Her decay brought her no sorrow; for she had glimpsed the secrets of the universe, her purpose for existence, but it died with her as her quarks scattered and recombined in all directions.

In her last instant, Penelope found herself wondering what they were all so scared of. For a moment, I became Truth, she thought. For a moment, I knew. I understood. With that, she dissolved completely, her quarks sifting into the fabric of the subatomic particles continuing to race around The Chamber in their wonderful frenetic dance of transformation.

PROTON IN THE FAST LANE
BY JADE YOUNG
ANTHROPOLOGY MAJOR (1998)

I was a disaffected proton when I was in whole form on this earth, just like you my friend. I am writing this short and sweet memoir from beyond my own dissemination, so that you may know the secrets that lay beyond the great collider.

I was living a dismally banal existence, wedded to a minuscule of a particle electron in holy hydrogen atomdom. I mean, when you are so much more massive than your mate, you are bound to be looking for something more exciting. Yeah, there was the electromagnetic attraction, but I was looking for something more like me. But even still, I knew this was a hopeless attempt at finding any meaning in my life; I had seen vicious love triangles between protons, pions, and neutrons, and I knew I was destined for something better than that. Life was too short, I'd seen kaons live barely long enough to experience the dreariness of this world, a lifetime of only 10^{-8} seconds.

I roamed the bad end of town, seeking out a life of mindless debauchery, but my little electron followed me wherever I went. It was a drag. Everything I saw around me was happening: particles were hooking up, forming atoms; the electricity was everywhere. But still there was the sadness, the decay, and the strangeness of it all.

Weak Force hustlers where promising all those they could get within their range a change in life, "We'll change the flavor of your quarks!"

I'd seen it done, they had some tricks up their sleeve, but I'd also seen the horrible decay they could cause. Oh, the madness of it all! No matter what interaction you could find yourself in, no matter what quarks you discovered living inside your soul, it was all the same: ups, downs, antiups, antidowns, strange. Hell, I'd even seen enough charm quarks and bottom quarks not be too excited anymore.

You could call me pessimistic, even depressive, but so was my life, I did not want to end up like the others; I wanted to be something BIG.

I hung out with a rag-tag group of cronies who felt just as pathetically miserable as I, and who sought out any fast escape from it. Particles kept joining our group, but it was only because particles were constantly going off and finding that ultimate mind-blowing experience. We were thrill seekers, and haunted all the known collider joints. My electron never approved of it.

"You better not be hanging out with those good-for nothing protons, running around in those sleazy accelerators! You're just waiting to leave me, I know it!" The poor old electron would spin off crazier than ever, wailing about my impending demise.

In the beginning, when we were first discovering realities beyond the walls of our nucleus, we protons were influenced by the great teachings of the East, and turned inward. It was a time of great experimentation, and our mad searching led to explosive results. Those before us were the first to try out the new colliders, and their collisions brought about the discovery that there is more to us than we first thought. There were quarks inside of us! It was a hard thing to do, to volunteer to annihilate oneself, but we were looking for the ultimate experience, taking us to speeds we never felt before, and letting us look at the brink of our own death. The thought was exhilarating, and I couldn't wait for my turn.

Our older buddies had gone out to The Linac, a kind of behind the times joint, but it always fired you up for one good run. But the service was slow, and the place simply didn't have the beam energy we were looking for. There had been a whole new string of colliders in the past years that were built with energy in mind called Synchrotrons. Instead of just shooting you through a straight line of electric fields, and then shooting you out at the end for a collision, the synchrotron would continuously loop you through a circular tube accelerator. This gave you more energy and prepared you for a collision with your antiparticle. They were fast, I thirsted for the experience, but I held off from volunteering. I knew something better was coming, and something inside of me told me to wait for that day. Providence came our way the year of 1995 in the Illinois quadrant. A new club was attracting all the boldest protons and antiprotons; it was called the Tevatron. Man, it was hot; all the young and lusting protons like us were showing up there. Something inside of me leaped when I heard the name, and I knew I was destined to go.

The Tevatron was a first-class joint, it used 1,000 superconducting magnets and it offered the highest beam energy anywhere, we're talking one trillion electron volts. With that amount of energy, it could accelerate us close to the speed of light. This was most delicious news, and I headed off to The Tevatron, my electron silent the whole way there. We both knew our life as a wedded hydrogen atom was near its end.

The place was packed and we were shoved into a container with other hydrogen atoms. The room was churning and in a second we were pushed into the accelerator. Everything was so confusing and exciting, and then I felt a wrench. I sped into a linear accelerator so quickly; I just barely caught a glimpse of my electron behind some screen, sadly spinning a goodbye to me. I was on my way and the speed was exhilarating. The linear accelerator ended and we entered the main hall of the Tevatron. My speed increased dramatically, and I felt higher than I've ever felt. My consciousness started to quiver, my reality blurred, I was approaching the speed of light.

As everything turned brilliant auras, I felt an ominous feeling of my own mortal form. And in the smallest fraction of a unit of time, I finally saw my death. It was beautiful, glorious, and I felt the mysteries of the world descend upon me. My partnered antiproton was also looking down upon our collision, as we exploded. Out of the collision there rose the greatest sight I ever did see: it was gigantic, massive beyond any elementary particle. I had never seen it before, but it was about 200 times more massive than I had been.

(Dear reader, I am sure that you know what that beautiful collision was all about that day in '95. The first top quark was discovered, completing the standard model of elementary particles. I am writing to you about my experience, because I know there are probably a lot of particles out there who feel like their existence has no special purpose. I was like you. You have to believe in whatever mysteries are in your essence. Who knows, maybe your soul houses unknown secrets that will change the path of physics.)

INTERVIEW WITH A PROTON
BY CHRISTINA LOMASNEY (1992)
RUSSIAN MAJOR

I had the great opportunity one day to speak to a proton about his own world that he calls the Subatomic Zoo. He told me all about the rules of the particle world, and about the reactions and decays that they regulate. This is the information that he gave me on our interview of May 8, 1992.

I was born during the great explosion of '92. Some people call it the Big Bang. I came from some energy along with my anticousin (we went our separate ways after the explosion and I haven't seen him since). My name is Proton and I want to tell you about the Subatomic Zoo that I live in. I have lots of relatives who came from energy also. Our friend the photon helped us to emerge from the energy, and we became known as the leptons and the hadrons. I myself am a hadron. Now I must clarify. Not all of my friends came about directly from the energy. Some came from the decays of others. You see, some of us don't live very long, but we don't totally die either.

We have laws about dying around here. For example if you want to die, you have to die into something else (it can be more than one thing) that has less mass than you, and you must conserve charge, baryon number, lepton number, and strangeness. Let me try to explain these things. First of all in our Subatomic Zoo we don't have social classes like you do, so we have to be classified by such things as our baryon number, strangeness, and charge. These things tell us who we can interact with, and who we can decay into. Baryon number is for baryons only, and everyone who is a baryon gets a +1. I am a baryon. Leptons have zero baryon number, (and so do mesons) but we compensate for that by giving them a lepton number. All Leptons get a +1 or a -1 lepton number, and we baryons get 0. Strangeness is another quality that we hadrons get. It depends on our quarks (the things that baryons and mesons are made of). You get your strangeness value from the strange quarks are inside of you. There is a relatively new member of our family, Omega, who has a strangeness of -3.

Now charge is very different because leptons and hadrons alike can have it. It tells us how we can interact. We cannot go near particles that have the same charge as us (except in special cases that I will explain later), but when we get together with someone of the opposite charge, we stick like glue (like the saying; opposites attract).

There are forces that act on us too. One is called the electromagnetic force. It controls how we behave when near (or far from, as its reach is infinite) another particle with charge. There is also a force called gravitational, but we particles don't really react very much to that one because the intensity of the gravitational force depends on how big we are and how much we weigh. Since we are very small, the graviton doesn't come around us very often. The graviton is the one that helps the gravitational force to do its work. Next there is the strong force. The strong force can over power the electromagnetic force. The strong force is what keeps other protons and I from repelling each other inside the nucleus (this is a place where I go sometimes with other protons and neutrons). It keeps protons and neutrons together so we can stay stable. Stable means that our system won't decay. I am proudly the only hadron that never decays. Neutrons are stable when they are with me in the nucleus, but when they leave the nucleus, they can only live for about 15 minutes.

We have another property that I'd like to tell you about. It is called spin. Leptons all have spin of 1/2. Baryons (the hadrons that are made of three quarks) all have spins that are multiples of 1/2 (this number is determined by the kinds of quarks that are inside of us and what they are doing). Mesons (the hadrons that are made of one quark and one antiquark) on the other hand have spins of 0 or some integer.

Before going any further into the explanation of our subatomic interactions, I would like first to explain to you the concept of the quark. Quarks, as I have mentioned, are what we hadrons are made of. If you are a baryon, you have three of the 5 kinds of quarks (there are actually 6 kinds of quarks, but one of them, top, doesn't like to be seen in public very often). I am going to concentrate on telling you about three kinds of quarks, up down and strange, and their anticousins. I am made of two ups and a down, and my anticousin that I told you about in the beginning of my story is made of two antiups and an antidown. My nucleus friend, the neutron, is made of two downs and an up. Another relative of mine, the lambda, is made of and up, a down and a strange (this is why she has a strangeness of -1). We never mix quarks and antiquarks in our make-up, so we are either made of only quarks or only antiquarks.

The mesons, on the other hand always mix quarks and antiquarks. They only have two objects in their make-up though. The pi+ for example is made of an up and an antidown. The other mesons follow the same general form. Quarks can never be found free, they are always bound inside of a hadron, because the force that binds them together gets greater as they are pulled apart.

The strong force also has the ability to rearrange quarks, and do pair production and annihilation through the mediator called the gluon. The weak force has the same abilities as the strong force, but it can also change a single quark type into another single quark type. The weak force is a force that I forgot to mention, but it acts on quarks as well as on leptons. The helpers of the weak force are the W^+, W^-, and Z^0 (which one actually helps depends on the charges that are being transferred). So in other words when we hadrons decay into other things, what is actually happening is that our inner quarks are being rearranged and/or changed.

Now I told you that there are basically only six types of quarks that you deal with in your everyday life, but that is not totally true. Those six quarks are divided into sub units with different colors. Now this quality was given to the quarks because of this exclusion rule that we have. You may know it as the Pauli Exclusion Principle. It states, (and I quote) "no two identical particles can be in the exact same state of energy and spin at the same time in the same body..." We had to give out the quality of color in order to help out particles like the omega that have three of the same quarks in their makeup.

Our physical properties state that only colorless particles are allowed to exist and in order to be colorless you must either be made up of one of each of the three colors (red, blue, and green), or you must be made of a color and the same anticolor. So, in other words this means that there are 36 quarks and antiquarks in total. The helper of the strong force that also holds quarks together (the gluon) also has colors that correspond to the interaction that they mediate.

Now that you have a feel for the things that make up our zoo, I would like to explain how we interact with each other. We have a lot of fun colliding with each other and turning into other things. We, of course, abide by all the rules of collision, and we always conserve charge, momentum, baryon number and lepton number. People sometimes enjoy forcing us to collide. For example, sometimes they'll collect some of my antiproton cousins and send them down a tube, and send me in the other direction. Then they watch what happens when we meet at the middle. It's actually a little more complicated than that. First, if we want really extensive reactions to occur, we need to supply a lot of energy to the reaction system. The best way to do this is for us to gain a lot of speed. We can't accelerate to the necessary speeds on our own, so people place us in electric fields. These make us speed up really fast (those of us with a charged nature anyway).

There are lots of different kinds of accelerators, as these are called, that function on different principles. First, there is a linear collider that employs the basic principle that I explained above. Next there is a circular collider that produces the highest energy collisions yet. Two oppositely charged particles are accelerated in opposite directions, so when we collide, our collision energy equals the sum of both of our acquired energies. Of course nothing compares to the energy from the Big Bang, but people are trying to simulate the energy levels that were available during the Big Bang so that they can observe particles like the top quark (he is the one who doesn't come out unless there are really high energies available).

People don't always like to observe us hitting each other though, sometimes they like to observe our decay processes, and see what kinds of things we can decay into. They use other machines for this purpose. The linear accelerator is the most basic kind of accelerator. We are accelerated in a straight electric field, getting energy boosts along the way. At the end there is a target (and sometimes a magnet) that we are forced to hit. The detection devices allow people to determine our nature by the way we react to the target, and by the way that we bend in the magnetic field. Synchrotrons are also fun. We get to go around and around the circle many times and each time around we have more energy. We eventually get released from the circle and get to run into another target. Then our reactions are measured. As of this time there is a very cool new project that people are working on. They want to build this really big new collider called the super-conductor super collider (SSC). It will bring us to immense energy levels and then collide us, and who knows what might happen then! Maybe the top will come out more often when there is so much fun to be had.

Editor's note: This story was written before Congress voted to cancel the SSC and before the top quark was discovered.

Stories

Fairytales

Fairytales

ONCE UPON AN ATOM
BY CAITLIN DAVENPORT FEELEY (1998)
FILM MAJOR

Deep in the hundred-acre wood lived a happy nuclear family. You could tell that strong forces held the Nucleon family together. They had pet gluons running around the house, from proton to proton, neutron to neutron, neutron to proton. Or at least they thought they had pet gluons; there were empty bowls, chewed bones and other compelling evidence, but the Nucleons never actually saw them. Anyway, one day, the parents, the neutrons, told their children, the three little protons, that it was time for them to go out into the world and seek their fortunes. In other words, they were tired of their kids sponging off them. The three Protons were a little surprised at this, as their parents were usually so neutral about everything. But, as always, the protons kept their positive outlook on life, and struck out on their own.

Peter Proton went off to Brookhaven, NY, where he found a whole group of other protons just like him! They shared a studio apartment in the Cosmotron. Patrick Proton went off to Berkeley, and found a similar commune in the kingdom of Bevatron. But Paula Proton, being more of a loner, decided she'd rather live all by herself, in Waxahachie, Texas. Her two brothers couldn't quite understand why she wanted to live alone in such a big, empty, abandoned place. They just thought she was silly.

Until, of course, that fateful day, when the big bad antielectrons came to town. These particles, also known as the Positron Gang, marched right up to the Cosmotron.

"Protons, Protons, let us come in!" they roared.

"Not by our quarks or our 1/2 spin!" cried the protons.

"Then we'll turn on this antiproton beam and blow you into little tiny bits! " And the big bad antielectrons did, before the protons could so much as say "Hey, that didn't rhyme."

Meanwhile, in Waxahachie, Paula Proton bolted up in her bed. "There is a great disturbance in the Force," she

85

said. "As if a million protons cried out in agony, and were silenced in a sudden burst of gamma radiation." When later, she felt the same disturbance; she knew that both her siblings had been annihilated. Finally, the big bad antielectrons came for her too.

"We'll turn on this antiproton beam and blow you into little tiny bits!" they roared.

"Just try it, antimatter boy!" shouted Paula. And sure enough, the big bad antielectrons could not turn on the beam.

"You fool!" shouted one of the older antielectrons. "Didn't you know the government killed the funding?" As they argued, Paula slipped out of the collider and fled home to her parents.

But when she got home, she found Weak Force Wolverines ripping her parents to pieces! Protons, electrons, and neutrinos flew everywhere! The horror!

"Get lost, you jackals! " cried Paula. She kicked one of the wolverines, but only hurt her foot because he was so massive. The wolverines fled, but it was too late. The neutrons were gone and the radioactive stench of beta decay hung thickly in the air.

"I must avenge the deaths of my siblings... but how?" Paula declared. "The big bad antielectrons repel me so; I can't even get near them."

"Why don't you journey to the Quarakle?" asked a voice.

"Of course! I shall consult the Quark Council. Who better to answer my questions but the most basic building blocks of my being! Who said that, anyway?"

"Me," said the voice. "I am Winnie the Pion. I am a particle of very little mass and an even shorter lifespan. I go from place to place, searching for nucleons to carry the Strong Force to. Now that I've found you, where are all the other nucleons?"

"They're dead. Slaughtered, decayed or annihil—."

"Oh Bother," said Pion, and he decayed, leaving only a very confused neutrino, and a muon that wandered off mooing into the woods.

"Just like a Meson," sighed Paula. "Leave it to us baryons to get things done..." And off she went in search of the Quarakle. After many months of traveling, she came to their hidden sanctuary in the mountains.

"Oh most wise and powerful six quarks, guardians of the mysterious power known as Color, please tell me how I may avenge the deaths of my family."

"First," a rather odd looking quark said, "you must strip down to the most simple, fundamental particles in order to understand your predicament."

"Look, I didn't come here for strangeness, old man," said Paula. "Are you gonna help me or what?"

"Patience, young hadron," said another quark. "For if you are to defeat the enemy, then you must understand his most basic characteristics, and thereby his weaknesses."

"I do not doubt that you speak the truth, wise one, but I do not understand."

"Ah, but the beauty of it is, you can destroy the enemy by introducing him to his opposite," said another quark. "We have the ancient knowledge of joining quarks and antiquarks to create mesons. But positrons are less virtuous beings. Should you join antielectrons with electrons, they will destroy themselves as they destroyed your siblings."

"But where am to find particles with such selfless honor, such negative charge?"

"Why, my dear young particle," said yet another quark, his voice oozing charm. "We would be glad to help you. Shall we summon some help for the fine young lady?"

"Why, yes, said two voices from a single proton floating nearby. And suddenly, two up quarks and a down quark emerged from their hiding and spoke the magic words:

"Three is one, and one is three;
The baryon's blessing, go with thee."

And as the words were spoken, The Seven Electrons appeared, looking like they just stepped out of a Kurosawa movie. "The Electron Kamikaze Squad awaits your orders!" they said.

"Are you quite certain you want to do this?" asked Paula. She was surprised, but she found these new particles strangely attractive.

"Of course! Are we not the anathema of our enemy? Are our spins and masses not as one? Are our charges not opposite? We shall strike them down and avenge the deaths of our masters, the Nucleons, around whom we circled so diligently and yet we could not protect! Besides, we'd have to be jailed for failing to protect our nucleus anyway. This sounds more fun than that."

"Very well, then," said Paula, as she led her new allies to Waxahachie. She knew that the big bad antielectrons would be lying in wait for her.

Subatomic bards would sing for many fractions of a second about that fateful battle. But in the end, the valiant and loyal electrons were destroyed along with the big bad antielectrons, in a great final flash of energy. From that energy were born young protons, who Paula adopted as her new younger brothers and lived with at the joint funded accelerator at CERN. And the newborn antiprotons were shipped C.O.D. to the particle beam back in Brookhaven. And so it was that Paula lived happily ever after with her newfound family, and that the Waxahachie accelerator was saved from the grip of the Positron Gang. Thus, particle physicists everywhere recall this tale of heroism and sacrifice, and point to the abandoned super collider so as to remind us. "Even in the darkest hour," they say, "Whether your family has been annihilated, or your funding cut off, there is still hope. Remember, there is no place like CERN."

ALICE'S ADVENTURES IN SUBATOMIC LAND
BY C. S. MITCHELL (2002)
PHILOSOPHY MAJOR

Alice let out a very long sigh as she shifted in her uncomfortable wooden chair, struggling to pay attention to her teacher who was going on and on about Russia and the Avant Garde.

"Really," thought Alice, "how can such wonderful works of art be so incredibly boring to talk about?"

As she waited for the teacher to fix the slide projector that had suddenly broken in the middle of the lecture, Alice decided to excuse herself to the restroom while no one was looking. She was heading down the hall towards the bathroom when she noticed that someone had been setting up for a small reception. There were cookies and tea and soda and crackers and at the very end of the table there was a small chocolate cake with the words "eat me" written on it in icing. Deciding to take this advice, Alice looked to the right, then looked to the left, and when she saw that no one was coming she helped herself to a big piece of the cake and hurried off to a secluded area where no one would see her eat the stolen cake.

"What a curious feeling," thought Alice after taking a few bites. She could tell that something was happening but she wasn't sure what. Alice walked back through the hallway and into a room where a student was trying to get a copy machine to work. With the final bite of the cake still in her mouth Alice cried "Oh dear!"

Alice gasped. She couldn't believe her eyes for it appeared that the student was beginning to grow at an alarming rate.

"Goodness gracious!" exclaimed Alice. "I should think if he grows any larger his head would go right through the ceiling!" But he kept growing larger and larger until he was finally so large that she could no longer see him. Alice took a few steps backwards in astonishment when she suddenly bumped right into someone.

"Watch where you're going!" it said.

"Oh I'm terribly sorry," said Alice.

"And by the way, he's not growing bigger," said the strange creature shortly. "You're shrinking." He paused for a second, and then, to be extra condescending for no apparent reason added, "obviously."

"But why, …? Where am I? Who are you?" asked Alice, taking a small step forward.

"I'm a neutron," he replied. "And if you don't mind I have to go now. I only have 923 seconds left to live, thanks to the seven seconds I just wasted talking to you!"

The neutron turned on his heel but before he could leave Alice exclaimed "A neutron! But that must mean, I must be..."

"A lot smaller than you were a few minutes ago. Look, I've got a lot to do and not a lot of time to do it, so if you'll excuse me now, I only have 917 seconds left to live!"

"What a peculiar creature," thought Alice. Seeing as he had a very short temper she decided not to bother him any longer. "I shall take the information he has given me and figure this out on my own," she decided to herself.

"Now let's see. I am very small now, and I wasn't very small before I decided to eat that cake. Even though I am not terribly fond of my class, I suppose it would never do to stay this small forever. If I eat more of this cake... oh no, that would probably make me even smaller and then I could never get back to my class. I suppose if I were to eat any more cake there would be nothing left of me at all."

Just then Alice heard a voice but she could not see the person who was talking.

"But that's not true," said the passing voice. "I'm a lepton and if you eat another piece of that cake, you can be as small as me."

"But I can't even see you," Alice replied. "How could I possibly know if I would want..."

But before she could finish, the neutron Alice presumed had already left, stumbled by and shouted "It's useless talking to point particles, little girl, they don't even have any mass!"

"I do so have mass! I'm just not made of anything smaller like you and your down quarks!"

"And an up quark thank you very much!" shouted the neutron. "And thanks to you I now only have 832 seconds left to live! I'd appreciate it if you'd stop talking to me now."

"You don't even have any charge!" the lepton taunted him. "Why don't you go turn into a proton, electron, and an antielectron neutrino or something!"

"You're just lucky I wouldn't hit anyone 1/1800th my size or I'd knock you into your next energy state!"

"Try me!"

"Okay, so I can't actually do that but, but, hey, stop looking at my quarks!"

Alice, fed up with listening to the lepton and the neutron argue, decided to keep walking in hopes of finding some more helpful particles. It wasn't long before she ran into another particle who was quick to introduce himself.

"Hello there girl. I'm one of the mediators of the weak force, you can call me W⁻. "

"Pleased to meet you," said Alice, and then quietly added, "you certainly are strange."

"Actually no. Say, you haven't seen a neutron around recently have you, dark hair, neutral charge, kind of surly?"

"Actually yes, I just left one a few minutes, er seconds, uh, I think something's wrong with my watch," Alice admitted and was pleased that the W⁻ ignored her confusion.

"Great, thanks" he replied and turned to leave.

"Wait," Alice stopped him, "You don't know where I could find someone to help me, you see I ate this cake, and I, I know you're quite busy, but..."

"Well now let me see, some of the strange particles are having a mixer just down the way."

"A mixer?" asked Alice.

"They all have very short lifetimes, much shorter than your neutron friend, so usually the sigmas and the lambdas especially like to have a few mixed drinks before they decay."

"Oh," said Alice, still a little confused. "So um, how do I get there?"

"If you're positively charged you can take that electric field over there, it's pointed in the right direction. If you're negative or neutral though, looks like you'll have to walk. Gotta go."

Alice stood puzzled in front of the electric field. Before she could even think to herself, "Why is there an electric field right here where I shrank in the copy machine room?" she noticed a woman moving closer and closer to the field.

"Pardon me but..."

"Not charged eh?" said the friendly proton who had apparently helped little girls who ate cake and were shrunken to subatomic sizes get to strange particle parties before. "Hold on and I'll take you there."

Alice was too tired and confused to question the proton so she grabbed hold, and was accelerated with the proton until they finally reached the party. She thanked the proton politely before they parted ways, and then decided to mingle. Just then a member of the kaon family handed her a drink.

"Here, drink this," he said. But before she could ask him what it was he disappeared leaving an extremely confused positive muon and muon neutrino in his place.

"What on earth!" exclaimed Alice. Just then the proton who had helped her earlier said, "That was a positive kaon. His lifetime is only about 10^{-8} seconds, sometimes less, so I wouldn't feel too bad if he didn't stick around and talk to you."

"Oh," said Alice, who then absent-mindedly threw back the drink that kaon had handed to her. Then, just as Alice was about to go off in search of a chaser, the proton continued to talk. Alice, grateful for her help earlier, found herself listening politely though her throat burned.

"Yeah, it's a shame. The other strange particles don't live long either. Lambdas, sigmas, even cascades don't live very long. Poor little baryons. Quite unstable."

"Yes," agreed Alice though she had no idea what the proton was talking about. "Poor kaon baryons and the like."

"No no, kaons are mesons, they have integer spins, the other strange particles are baryons because they have half integer spins," said that proton beginning to sound like the angry neutron.

"Oh yes, integer spins and particles and lifetimes and such. So...do you have spin?" asked Alice, deciding it was less rude to ask this question than to ask whether protons are stable or not.

"I do, my spin is 1/2. I also have a positive charge," she said proudly. "And, not only—" She stopped abruptly and gave Alice a disappointed and yet somewhat sympathetic look.

"Look's like I won't get to finish talking with you," she said.

"But why?" asked Alice, getting a little nervous by her change in tone.

"Look behind you."

Alice turned around slowly and saw the strangest thing she had ever seen before in her life. Herself. Or was it herself? A little girl who looked almost exactly like Alice stared right back at her. For a moment Alice thought she might be looking into a mirror.

"Who are you?" asked Alice, trembling.

"I'm an antiAlice. Come here a second, I want to tell you something."

Alice didn't move. "But, what..." she hesitated. "What are you?"

"I'm your antiparticle. I have the same mass as you, and no charge because you have no charge, but the properties you have that can have opposites,"

"Yes..." Alice prompted her.

"Well, I have those properties. The opposites, I mean. Now seriously, I need you to come here for just a minute."

Alice, having no idea that instant annihilation could be in her near future, but nevertheless scared out of her wits at the mere prospect of an antiself, began to run. AntiAlice ran after her yelling, "It's not like it's going to hurt or anything, come back here!"

"She'll annihilate you," offered the proton watching the whole thing with a small amount of interest.

Alice, not too keen on being annihilated, began to run faster.

"Come on, Alice! This is our chance to really do something, to do something great! We can make energy you and I! Stop trying to fight it!"

For some unknown reason the antiAlice ran out of breath and decided to catch up with Alice later. Alice heaved a sigh of relief and decided to leave the strange particle mixer once and for all (which incidentally, is not to suggest that strange particles are necessarily mixing with each other but rather that they like drinking mixed drinks, which makes a lot more sense).

Just then Alice saw several neutrinos sitting around eating pork chops and applesauce. One of them was telling a story very enthusiastically.

"And they were all scared and like, we'd better get out of here, and I was all like, whatever, I'm not afraid of gluons, and they're all like but it's the strong force, and I'm like, whatever I'm not afraid of the strong force, I mean, come on man, as long as I don't see any Z's or W's or whatever I'm not even..."

Alice decided not to investigate and kept on moving. After walking a little while longer and not running into anyone or anything Alice began to get nervous. "Now where am I?" she wondered. There didn't seem to be anyone for miles, or millimeters, or much less because Alice really wasn't sure just exactly how small she was. She used her fingers to try to figure it out, reasoning, "If I started out about four feet tall, and now I'm much smaller, hmmm".

Just then she noticed a small flask with the words, "Drink Me" written on a tiny little label. But before Alice could drink it she was bombarded by an alpha particle, which is really just a helium nucleus, and which really hurt because it was two protons and two neutrons and as the proton she talked to earlier was about her size, it was a lot like getting hit by four people at once.

"Ouch!" cried Alice. "That REALLY, REALLY hurt!"

"Sorry," replied one of the neutrons in the alpha particle. "We're not exactly enjoying this either. You see, um, where do I begin? Have you ever heard of polonium before?"

Alice, deciding she didn't want to hear anymore, drank the contents of the "Drink Me" bottle hoping that it would make her return to her normal size. Instead, however, she turned into a bottom quark which is a really big disappointment when you're hoping to become a normal sized human again. But Alice, being a relatively optimistic person and highly adaptable figured it wasn't so bad. Besides, now she at least had a charge (-1/3) and was five times bigger than a proton, which though she really couldn't explain why, was somehow gratifying.

Fairytales

JACK DIRAC AND THE BEANSTALK; A PHYSICIST'S FAIRYTALE.
BY JONG SOO KIM (1990)
ENGLISH MAJOR

Once upon a time, there was a young lad named Jack Dirac. He was around the age of sixteen, and he was a very bright young man. He lived on a modest farm with his widowed mother, and they were very poor. They were once wealthy, but several years ago an evil force by the name of Gravity had come and "pulled" their life-savings from them. Gravity was a powerful and greedy man who had come into their town of Schwarzville, and he took anything that he was attracted to. Moreover, he had taken all of the Dirac family's belongings, and all they were left with was their land and their house.

To the villagers of Schwarzville, their diet was simple and boring because all they had to eat was three types of produce. They certainly knew that other varieties existed; however, these were the only ones that had been discovered so far. The vegetables were called electron-beans. The fruits were called proton- honeydews and neutron-cantaloupes. Jack grew all three in his modest garden. This small garden was the only source of income for him and his mother. The produce was planted in rows with the row of neutron-cantaloupes strategically planted between the other two. This was necessary because when the electron-beans were planted next to the proton-honeydews, they would, by some twist of nature, extend their long plant roots to the honeydews and try to pull them closer to their bean bodies. Jack was perplexed by this, but he noticed that the electron-beans grew properly when placed next to the cantaloupes for they did not deem to react to this neutral fruit at all. Jack was a good gardener and tended to his fruits and vegetables every day. Jack and his mother sold them to their neighbors, and the earnings helped them live with some comfort.

One day, Jack was in an intense conversation with his three best friends: Albert Einstein, Max Planck, and James Maxwell. As usual, they were discussing their current farming theories. Each was trying to discover new types of produce by coming up with such innovative ideas as electromagnetic water, relativity theory, and some absurd quantum vegetable that could grow from one place to another instantly with no roots. Jack Dirac listened carefully to his knowledgeable friends, and he let these interesting ideas swim around in his head. For days he thought about all that his friends had told him. Maybe there was a way to put it all together. Maybe electromagnetic water would not work alone. Perhaps the exact locations didn't matter but the relative placements did. Maybe the quantum vegetable placed properly and watered correctly were the key to future farming success.

That night, Jack had the most unusual dream. He dreamt that he had discovered a new strain of vegetable called the positron beanstalk. By growing one huge beanstalk from only one seed, he had produced thousands of beans that he then sold to the villagers at low prices. He became a very rich man, and he saved his mother from the grips of poverty.

When Jack awoke from this dream, he quickly went about the task of creating such a strain of vegetable. After years of investigating and testing various bean plants, he thought that he had finally come up with the perfect strain of bean. It was opposite to regular electron-beans; it was like some sort of antielectron bean. It needed little sunlight, little care, and it would grow to tremendous heights. He planted the seed and watered it with a few drops of Electromagnetic brand water (which is specially formulated to affect vegetables which have an actual charge). Suddenly, the plant began to grow and it would not stop growing. Jack was so amazed by the discovery and he became quite curious about how high the beanstalk was. So he decided to climb it.

Meanwhile, the evil Gravity, who had heard about Jack's amazing beanstalk, had become jealous because he believed that Jack and his mother might gain much good fortune, and he wanted some of it too. So he hurried over to Jack's garden. To his surprise, he saw the biggest, greenest beanstalk that he had ever seen. He looked up and saw Jack climbing about twenty meters above. He shouted after him, but Jack continued to climb because he knew that Gravity was evil. Gravity tried to "attract" Jack to come back down by bribing him with candy, yet luck did not prevail for this sinister man. Therefore, Gravity decided to go up the beanstalk. Unfortunately for him, this soon proved to be a powerful mistake. They climbed higher and higher: 50 meters, 100 meters, and 200 meters. As they went farther away from the ground, Gravity felt weaker, but he was determined to be involved in any further discoveries. Suddenly, he was so weak that he lost his grip and slipped. He fell and spiraled to the ground. To the delight of the villagers of Schwarzville, the evil Gravity was finally dead! Nevertheless, Jack continued to climb.

Finally he came to the top of the beanstalk and he gasped at what he saw. He had never laid his eyes on such a sight before. It was a whole new land that existed above the clouds. Everywhere he looked he saw vegetables that he had never seen in his life. It was every young farmer's paradise. He had discovered and named the neutrino-carrot and the antineutrino-carrot, the muon-lettuce and the antimuon-lettuce, the antiproton-honeydew and the antineutron-cantaloupe and the anti, neutral, and pion-watermelons. The antifruits and antivegetables were the opposite versions of the same items. They would grow longer, need less sunlight, and less water. Jack quickly took his discoveries back home to his mother.

She was proud of her son and soon became a happy woman again. They decided to expand their fruit and vegetable stand to include these new fruits and vegetables and to offer them to the villagers of Schwarzville. They decided to give their products name brands. They sold all their fruits under the name of Hadron and all of their vegetables under the name of Lepton. However, they first had to grow these vegetables and fruits before they could sell them. After some experimentation, Jack and his mother found that Hadron fruits responded best to Strong Force brand water. Out of the vegetables, the muon lettuces were the only ones that tended to decay after they were removed from the garden. All of the fruits, except the proton honeydews, tended to decay after picking. But this was not a problem because the villagers bought and ate them very quickly. The villagers were so impressed by these new additions to their diet that they devoured these interesting and wonderful foods.

Thus, Jack Dirac and his mother became very rich. Without the discovery of the positron-beanstalk, Jack would not have been led to the discoveries of Hadrons and Leptons. Thus, they earned more money than they needed, never to become poor again. Jack Dirac and his mother lived happily ever after.

Editor's note: In 1931, Paul Dirac, seeking to unify the theories of Albert Einstein, Max Planck and James Clerk Maxwell, predicted the existence of the positron, the antiparticle of the electron. It was discovered in 1932.

SNOW WHITE AND THE SEVEN (UH...SIX) QUARKS:
A FAIRY TALE FOR PHYSICISTS' CHILDREN
BY ELIZABETH WILLSE (1998)
ANTHROPOLOGY MAJOR

Once upon a time, there was a hardworking particle physicist named Snow White. She was named Snow White by parents who raised her in a commune and didn't know that she would go on to a career in scientific research, instead of raising goats. She worked at Fermilab, in the far-off land of Batavia. She had risen through the ranks there, from a humble graduate student to the lofty position of a senior experimental physicist. She was responsible for designing experiments that led to new discoveries.

Snow White didn't have anything to complain about, really. Except for one thing; or rather, one person. One of the other experimental physicists didn't like Snow White very much. Her name was Dr. Medeous and she really didn't have very good reasons for hating Snow White so much. Sometimes Snow White's experimental group got a few minutes more of beamtime. And, more often than not, they had just a few more events to use as proof for their conclusions. But really, that wasn't a reason for a senior physicist like Dr. Medeous to despise Snow White.

You see, word had been spreading around Fermilab that Dr. Medeous had spent maybe a little too much time getting exposed to synchrotron radiation, or watching tiny particles bump into one another. She'd been acting stranger and stranger in recent years. Her vendetta against Snow White was one aspect of her diminishing grip, on reality.

The way she had started talking to the Tevatron was another. Dr. Medeous had been talking to the Tevatron, Fermilab's proton/antiproton collider. Of course, it doesn't take a doctorate degree in particle physics to talk to machinery. People talk to computers and household appliances all the time. Swearing at a particle accelerator or begging it not to break down doesn't help any more than it helps to talk to a car or a computer, but it makes people feel better.

But Dr. Medeous had taken talking to inanimate objects to a whole new level. When she thought nobody was listening, she spoke to the Tevatron in rhymed couplets.

"Tevatron, Tevatron, where protons bump and race, how do I wipe that smirk off of Snow White's face?"

Of course, the Tevatron never really answered. It wasn't a magic mirror. The protons and antiprotons kept on racing around and around and bumping into each other, and computers kept on recording data (in between needing to be fixed, of course) and the only answer she ever really got was the aforementioned fact that Snow White's experiments were doing very, very well. And equipment never broke down during Snow White's shift in the lab.

Like her coworkers, Snow White had noticed Dr. Medeous's growing antipathy and shrinking sanity. She had taken to avoiding Dr. Medeous whenever possible.

One day, she saw Dr. Medeous stomping towards her, a particularly vicious scowl on her face. To avoid colliding with her nemesis, Snow White stepped through the first door she found, without bothering to read the sign on the door. Perhaps if she had read the sign, she would have decided that "Caution, Antiproton Storage Facility" was not an invitation to use that door as an escape route. And of course, doing so during an experiment's beam run was probably not wise. As it was, though, she stepped directly into the path of a stream of antiprotons moving at very, very high speeds.

She realized the minute the door closed behind her that she appeared to be standing in a meadow that was decidedly not the prairie surrounding Fermilab's facility. It took her a few moments to adjust to this turn of events and a few moments more to adjust to the sight of a small, rustic cottage and the two men who were bounding across the field towards each other. They slammed into each other, and fell onto the grass. When they stood up, there appeared to be an entire crowd of men. Snow White was dazedly trying to count them, when they rushed at each other again. Again they fell, their small bodies disappearing in the tall grass. And when they stood a second time, there were six of them. These six shook hands and stepped back.

One of the little men saw her. "Hello, pretty lady!" he called.

The others looked towards her, and then ran towards her. She was afraid they would crash into her as they had crashed into each other. Instead, they stopped a few feet away, and regarded her solemnly for a moment. Then one stepped forward.

"Hi! I'm the Top quark around here! Welcome to our domain!" he said.

She shook his hand automatically, even as she wondered where she was and her keen physics intellect rebelled against the impossibility of her current situation.

"I'm Snow White," she said, ignoring rational thought for the moment.

"Pleased to meet you, Dr. White," said another dwarf...no, quark, as he stepped forward and bowed low over her hand. He kissed the back of her hand in a chivalrous manner.

"Charmed, I'm sure, " she said dazedly.

He straightened up and winked at her. "Exactly!"

"So, you must be... Up, Down, Strange, and Beaut... err, Bottom."

She was not exactly sure which quark was which, but was willing to make a fair guess at the identity of at least two of them. The quark dressed in several colors of waning plaids and polka dots, topped with a Hawaiian shirt was decidedly odd. Even, perhaps, strange. And the last quark she had named bore a distinct resemblance to Antonio Banderas.

"You can call me either Beauty or Bottom, it doesn't matter to me," said the Antonio Banderas look-alike quark. His voice was well modulated in the tones of a professional operatic tenor, or a classically trained Shakespearean actor, with just enough of a flirtatious tone to make Snow White blush.

"And, you're Up?" Snow White guessed, unlocking her gaze from that of the incredibly compelling beautiful quark and looking at one who hadn't introduced himself yet.

The quark that she addressed heaved a sigh that shuddered through his entire body.

"Nobody knows me. Nobody loves me. Everyone who comes here wants to meet the Charmed quark, the Strange, and the Beauty one. And even the Up. I don't rate a second look. I'm old news."

"Oh, you know that's not true!" scolded Top. To Snow White he said, with a shrug. "He's a Down. He's like this most of the time."

"And I'm an Up!" said the last quark, with a broad grin and a firm handshake.

"It's wonderful to meet all of you," said Snow White. She looked around. "So... you all live here?"

"More or less, " said Top. "As you know, it's hard for any Quark to stay stable for long. Weak forces and strong forces blow through here all the time," he said. He squinted up at the brilliantly blue sky. "Weather's been clear for a while, though. So we've gotten used to things being the way they are. We have our differences of opinion though, you know how that is, weeks where a couple of us can't stand the sight of the rest of us."

Snow White nodded, thinking of Dr. Medeous.

"Beauty and I, or Charm and Strange, or Up and Down and Strange, will go off sometimes too, to have kind of a Quarks Night Out and get away from the rest of the gang at Club Baryon, over that hill there."

"AARDVARK!" bellowed Strange. Up hushed him.

Snow White wasn't sure how to frame her next question. "Are... are you six the only partic... err, dwar... err quarks around here?"

Top guessed what she was trying to ask. "Oh yeah, there are antiquarks living here too. But they live far away from us, and we try not to get together with them very often. All hell breaks loose when we get together with them. That's how an earlier generation of our family ceased to exist. Got too close to the antiquarks."

"I'm sorry," said Snow White, feeling obligated to offer some form of sympathy, without knowing exactly what form it should take.

"Don't worry about it," Beauty chimed in. "As Top said, we're not terribly stable."

"The eggplants are crawling towards me!" shrieked Strange, wrenching himself out of Up's grasp and spinning across the field.

"And some of us are much less stable than others," Up said, shaking his head, while Snow White and the quarks tried not to snicker.

"There are unstable people too, back where I come from," Snow White said. "So I know exactly what you mean." She thought of the evil Dr. Medeous again.

Charm appeared at her side. "Is there someone troubling you, Milady? I can help! I'll save you!"

She smiled. "Thank you for offering, but no. I think I can handle this on my own. As a matter of fact, I should probably be getting back."

"Do you know how to get back?"

"Sure," said Snow White. "Just click my heels three times and say there's no place like Fermilab."

The quarks stared at her as though she were crazier than Strange.

Down said, "You're stuck here, for the rest of your life. You get to watch us decay. Maybe you'll start to decay too."

Up, still smiling cheerfully, smacked him. "No. All you have to do is find your antimatter and get close enough to it to begin a reaction."

"But... but... my antimatter is back in the lab! Dr. Medeous is probably stomping around looking for me, because her last conversation with the Tevatron told her that I was conspiring against her, even as we speak! How am I going to get her here so I can react with her?"

"Good point," said Top, looking thoughtful.

"Then stay here with us," said Beauty, offering his exquisitely shaped hand. Charm nodded. "You will be happy here."

"Much as I'd love to, I really have to get back. I'm going to try the Dorothy approach to getting out of here."

Feeling incredibly silly, Snow White began to click her heels together, repeating, "There's no place like Fermilab. There's no place like Fermilab."

"There's no place like Fermilab..."

Snow White jolted upright.

Her pale cheeks were creased red from the wrinkles of the paper she'd fallen asleep on. She was sitting at her desk, which was strewn with printouts and graphs and sketches. And she was late for a meeting to plan a conference panel.

She collected her papers and dashed down the hall, hoping that she wouldn't run into Dr. Medeous at the one time when she probably deserved a lavish scolding for her lateness.

As she pushed her way through the chatting physicists who stood in the hall, she bumped into a short, dark haired man. He turned to respond to her hasty apology. Snow White almost stopped in her tracks. The short scientist had looked very, very, much like Antonio Banderas. And he had winked at her.

A FERMI LAB FAIRY TALE
BY NAVIN RAJAGOPALAN (2002)
CHEMISTRY MAJOR

The land of Atmos was falling into ruin. King Proton was angry, not just slightly ticked, the way that you get when you stub your toe in the morning, but the smoldering rage that only a massive hadron could feel. It was a small kingdom, Atmos, only 0.000000001 dimensions, so when the King was mad everyone in Brookhaven County could hear. He huffed, he puffed, and he screeched and moaned, zipping around till he was as red as the color charge for the strong force.

"This is enough to make me change from up to down!" he cried (of course with those quarks he would be too much like his brother Neutron). Much to his chagrin, no one was paying much attention to him. Instead the focus was on determining how anyone could have broken into the castle. After all, the walls were made with strong force and the best gluons possible; it would have taken a lot of energy to get in. They consulted the Feynman log of all incoming and outgoing particles and their mediators...nothing was amiss. Some electrons had come and gone, releasing a photon, but this was perfectly normal. Queen Electron was orbiting nearby with the quiet grace and incredible speed accorded to a lepton of her stature. She stopped to pause by her husband just in time to catch him from a fainting spell. He spun around a little (as half integer spinners do) and then collapsed in her arms. The collision might have caused something if momentum was conserved, but she was stationary and there was too much activity around. The castle was abuzz with subatomic particles, tauons were falling apart in the span of 290 femto seconds (typical!), and tau neutrinos were skirting along practically invisible. The heavy siblings of electrons, the muons proceeded to break apart into two neutrinos and an electron within milliseconds of hearing the news. The nucleons were standing off to a side, the protons sandwiched between the neutrons of similar half integer spin and mass, while the lighter electrons rushed back and forth sometimes acting like waves and sometimes like particles. They were always so uncertain. Of the other leptons, the muons were the most active, coming from positive and negative pions along with neutrinos, only to then decay into electrons and positrons. Neutrinos were everywhere and antiparticles were being created in the heat of the moment (but they were captured soon enough or annihilated by kamikaze particles). Chaos was everywhere too, but then again, Atmos was falling into ruin…and Princess Cascade was missing.

Princess Cascade had always been a strange child; the doctors said it was due to her composition, one, too many strange quarks they said, probably from her volatile conception via the strong force. Strange particles were always an unusual breed, unstable and always produced in pairs. Sometimes King Proton thought that the only thing he shared with his daughter was their baryon number of one and half integer spin. She was too fleeting, too ephemeral to understand his place as a nucleon. Of course Proton took some consolation in the fact that his wife shared even less in common with their daughter. At least he could still communicate with her thanks to the gluons. Leptons and baryons were just so different. A neutron charged along to conserve momentum; time stood still and for one fleeting picosecond it seemed like order would prevail.

But then time moved backward, and we go from the land of Atmos to Antatmos where an equally worried King Antiproton and Queen Positron were attempting to find the missing Prince Anticascade. The two kings were bitter enemies. They had waged several wars and annihilated most of their armies, but still they would not end the fighting. So much energy had been wasted, but the army of antimatter was growing stronger. In the beginning there had been less of them and they had co-existed in a curious asymmetry, but now things were really different. The irony was that the two kingdoms were not really that different at all. King Proton has the same number of quarks and mass as King Antiproton. It is just their other properties (like baryon number and charge) that were completely opposite.

Of course the missing Prince Anticascade, did not help matters. "Its that damned Proton, he's behind this! I'll bet he snuck a virtual particle into the room and kidnapped our son, damn that quantum uncertainty!"

Queen Positron attempted to calm the King down, "You're always so negative, try to look at the positive for once" she crooned in her soft, temperate voice. "He might just have snuck out somewhere with his friends, you know how kids today are. Remember that time he went to the synchrotron track to race, he was accelerating so fast I thought he might have a collision…thank god for the controlled magnets." She broke out in a smile, but it was only half hearted, deep down she knew something was wrong, and Antatmos would never be the same again.

"Get my detectors!" boomed King Proton, "I want to know the charge, mass, velocity, energy and identity of every particle in Atmos, and there will be no rest until my daughter is found!"

Thousands of particles were galvanized; they used scintillating counters (an old and simple method but still quick), wire, drift and bubble chambers, Cerenkov counters; no expense was spared to construct tracking chambers with calorimeters specific to the Princess's unique energy signal. But to no avail, she was gone, and although they could follow her trail, it disappeared at the outskirts of Atmos (she probably used a neutral hadron to help cover her tracks). Meanwhile King Antiproton and Queen Positron were having just no better luck in finding Prince Anticascade. It was as if he had completely disappeared. Atmos and Antatmos were in ruin and there was only one thing to do: war would be declared. And so the armies of Atmos and Antatmos met, and fought. Energy was created and energy was lost but in the end the Prince and Princess were still missing. Finally after days of fighting a truce was declared, but still they could not find the particles. In specially designed electromagnetic chambers, the Royals of Atmos and Antatmos convened.

"What, what about the Dark Lands?" asked Queen Electron, worried. "Could they have gone there?"

"Impossible," scoffed King Antiproton. "No one has been to the Dark Lands. Its just a story to frighten little particles at night."

They sat there, all through the night, debating, searching, and thinking. When day broke the photons rushed in bringing news. The Princess had been spotted for just a few seconds on horseback, riding toward the outskirts of Atmos. Time stood still. Squarks and sleptons pushed by.

On a silky black hill Princess Cascade dismounted her horse and pulled her cloak back; she stretched out her hand and smiled. On that same hill Prince Anticascade reached out his hand and returned her smile. Strangers no more, they touched.

Time moved on, still neutrons rushed by, but the world had two fewer particles.

Poems

Poems

ODE ON THE DEATH OF A TOP QUARK
BY JOHN B. STONE (1997)
ENGLISH MAJOR

A quark has left our lives today;
an errant traveler in the quantum fray.
His life with us was but a moment brief,
Decay stole him away like a particle thief.
The twin child of a proton/ antiproton pair colliding
in the night
which came together with all the Tevatron's magnetic might.
From this cataclysmic annihilation,
came two lives as emanations.

In this passion Top was bred.
His charge was positive and his color red.
He was by far the largest quark to arise.
175 times a proton was his size.
Now with the Standard Model complete,
next to sister Bottom, he took his seat.
And to complement his particle throne,
this Top quark did not sit alone.

Top's brother born on this same day
was opposite from him in every way.
His charge was negative and on his head,
was laid the color antired!
From his parents' death he flew
in a different direction than his brother would do.
With his brother, he might have liked to abide
but conservation of momentum would not let him slide.

Alas, these two bright beings soon had to die,
though for a fraction of a second they did fly!
The weak force could not for long be denied
and so these two quarks fell in their pride.
But from this decay, nothing was truly lost
For the conservation of energy prevents such a cost.

From these decays, a legacy of particles was left
to replace the quarks of which we were bereft.

Those particles which fly off in jets,
for their poor parent they hold no regrets.
Hadrons and Leptons care nothing for their kin.
Their only concern is "fraction or integer spin?"
At incredible speeds they perpetually fly around
and for this death, they utter no compassionate sound.
Now, perhaps you might think that my image is bleak.
This is not how you imagine the particles named in Greek.

However, life in an accelerator is not sweet,
in a millionth of a second, a particle's life is complete.
The only things to record that one has been
is a particle detector and a student's pen.
I would never choose this world in which to be
with the strong and weak forces there to harass me
If you will, accept my words as true,
life's a jungle in the Subatomic Zoo.

PHYSICS DINNER
BY MEGUMI MATSUKI (2002)
UNDECIDED MAJOR

J.J. Thompson invited me to dinner.
His electron discovery was certainly a winner.
But the table was bare,
only champagne and glassware,
"Where's the food? I came to eat, not to leave thinner."

Then Thompson led me to a different dining hall.
I was greeted by physicists having a ball.
"That first room's for Future,
with new dishes from Nature."
Fashionably late, or maybe she'll time warp and surprise one
and all.

There was particle soup for the entire group,
A subatomic scoop I couldn't see with a loupe.
Astronomical fishes,
high-energy dishes,
A table of elements that could feed Augustus Gloop.

At last came the anticipated plum pudding dessert.
Embedded with electrons, the chef did assert.
We praised our host,
and said, "A toast!"
But then something made our attention divert.

Rutherford's alpha cake was making a ruckus.
It started shooting particles at the pudding and us.
Some crumbs went through,
others bounced back, who knew?
We were witnessing the discovery of the nucleus!

Poems

ODE TO FUNDAMENTALS
BY SALLY FRANKLIN (1995)
URBAN STUDIES MAJOR

What are we made of, can we make a conclusion?
One thing this story supports is the fundamental confusion.

In 1914 Rutherford played with radiation,
and the nucleus was discovered when alphas came back.
When he did it again with Chadwick and nitrogen,
hydrogen emerged and the proton came back fast.

Electrons and protons, that's what it's all about!
But someone cried "what about spin?"
And in 1932, atomic theory couldn't do without
the neutron to knock a proton through paraffin.

More radiation, let's play with beta decay!
But it doesn't conserve energy and momentum.
We can't throw two conservation laws away!
Perhaps a new particle needs to enter the equation.

So, in the 1920's Pauli had made a prediction
about another particle called the neutrino,
and Savannah River later made the difficult detection
of a particle that had charge and mass equal to zero.

But how, I often ask, can these things stay together?
And what are the forces that tear us apart?
Is it fate, animal magnetism, pheremones or the weather?
Interactions are complicated; what drives our hearts?

Fundamental forces control the reaction's destiny;
They are gravitational, electromagnetic, strong and weak.
And mediators run around, (in Feynman's diagrams we see):
they are gravitons, photons, W's and Z's.

So in this great search for the special One,
we have only found more fish in the sea;
and as the 30's, 40's and 50's spawned the great baby boom,
scientists increased the number of particles substantially.

Dirac started with the positron, which is the antielectron;
and they led us to the world of antimatter.
Cause with them came the antineutron and the antiproton
and also annihilation with some scatter.

Yukawa predicted the pion as a force carrier
by finding the mass from the range.
While it turned out the gluon's the force carrier,
our ideas about force and mass are changed.

But what do the pions decay into themselves?
They're muons, two to chose from, with neutrinos to match.
But another comes up as we further delve;
it is tau, with a neutrino, that in '75 they did catch.

By this time we had enough particles along
to place into groups of leptons and hadrons.
Hadrons deal with a force that is strong
and are composed of baryons and mesons.

Leptons are not strong force choosers
and have a half-integer spin,
while the baryons are also half-integer users
the meson is the integer spin champion.

In the 1950's , after the unstable pion was confirmed,
some new particles and properties were discovered.
Strangeness, the scientists soon learned,
could be applied to new particles that were uncovered.

Lambdas, sigmas, cascades and kaons,
they are all produced in pairs by the strong force.
Their decay sometimes left no trace of protons or neutrons,
and they are all unstable as a matter of course.

Strangeness, lepton number, and baryon conservation
were some new laws that the particles were catching.
A decaying particle must be more massive than the ending combination,
and neutrinos and leptons must always be matching.

Then in '64 quarks were introduced by Zweig and Gell-Mann
as fundamental particles which form hadrons.
They were up, down, and strange, and the antiparticles with them.
A quark and antiquark form mesons, and three form baryons.

More studies gave rise to the powers of forces strong and weak
to rearrange and annihilate the quarks into pairs and flavors.
And Brookhaven and SLAC found the charm to complete
the second generation of quark-lepton endeavors.

But the tau/antitau still had no match to make a third generation
for the standard model to be in symmetry.
Along with eight gluons, the graviton, the W, Z and photon,
the standard model needed the quarks called top and bottom.

In '95, the tau and antitau had finally found their mates
when Fermilab gave proof to the top quark's reputation.
Their collider learned from a detector that scintillates
of a particle that was naturally formed at the earth's creation.

The top has the mass of about 170 protons, and that
should give insight into the mass of every substance.
But with so many particles to wonder and marvel at,
it's not surpassing that we still can't explain our existence.

A TOPLESS GENERATION
BY MARY H. HANSEL (1993)
PSYCHOLOGY MAJOR

There once was a quark hypothesized and found,
but even for a bottom, she was awfully down.
She cried everyday, sighing and dragging her feet.
The source of her sadness: her generation was incomplete.

Her friend the proton, optimistic and bright
tried to cheer her up saying "You're lovely, quite a sight!"
Yet Bottom protested, she knew something was askew:
"I cannot feel beautiful without the truth!"

A tau neutrino listening nearby,
along with a negative tau, responded to her cry.
They admitted they too felt a gap in the standard model,
that must be filled, with no time to dawdle!

The first generation had its ups and downs, for sure,
but felt whole with its electron neutrino and electron pure.
A real charmer found with its evil twin from the Antimatter Zone
finished set two with a muon, neutrino, and strangeness all its own.

So away the three particles flew knowing just where to stop,
for anyone knows, every bottom needs a top!
Along their journey, the particles met some strange ones,
all hadrons experiencing the strong force – a drug they had done.

It was brought to them by its usual carrier, the gluon,
and the ways they spun made sigma, lambda, and kaon meson
They were not much help, as their spinning made them sick
but sober protons and neutrons, also part of the baryon clique,
directed Bottom and friend to Fermilab and CERN in Switzerland.
Apparently the physicists there could give the three a hand.

For it was there that she with her antibottom had been born.
She cried aloud the day she was torn
from the gluons and quarks that made up the soup,
everyone was poised for the top quark coup.

But neither Fermilab, nor CERN could seem to find the quark,
And the rest of the group was getting tired, as it was getting dark.

Yet they pushed on, showing their true colors, rising to the test,
red, green and blue, for together these yield colorless.
They had an idea to find particle accelerators:
Linac, synchrotrons, and two kinds of colliders.
Surely one of these would be able to create enough energy to
locate Bottom's mate.

They tried and they tried, using Einstein's equation,
but all were scared of Top's quick annihilation.
Finally, Eureka! Tau minus spotted the top
along with his antiparticle, but the two would not stop.

They were heading straight towards a hurling pion plus!
Bottom could not look, everyone was hushed.
But alas, they barely missed each other by just a nanometer!
Bottom was ecstatic as the pair then came to greet her.

Six leptons and six quarks, as theorists have proposed.
Top and Bottom hand in hand, and thus the search is closed.

Poems

PHYSICS IS PHUN
BY ALLISON BREN (1997)
ART MAJOR

Back in 1964, wide swung-open a Physics door!
"Gadzooks" cried Gell-Mann, "You won't believe it
but al l these particles are just three bits!"
Gell-Mann made a great discovery,
and spread it far to all and sundry!
He called on Joyce to help him name it
"Quarks" he yelled, "That's it, fantastic!"
He gave them each a measly charge
and left the quandary to the world at large.

But soon there grew to be a problem,
all the quarks could not be just one,
There had to be more balancing leptons!
More work was in store and it wouldn't all be phun!

The first individuals were up and down,
and soon the third quark "strange" was found.
But physicists hoped at least for four,
and searched their data a little more.

Sure enough, in seventy-four,
sun-loving Californians made a score.
They had good luck and found quark charm
but now the search was just getting warm!

In three more years, Bottom appeared–
it seemed the end was drawing near!
But then the physicists hit a bump,
on the search for top they were totally stumped.

The race for top was hard and long
in many labs accelerators hummed.
Physicist's were confounded by the particle's mass,
the guesses they'd made it far surpassed.

Now one lab had a special tool–
an accelerator called Tevatron they thought would rule.
Around this electro-magnetic racetrack,
raced antiprotons and protons, back to back.

Collisions occurred millions of times
and physicists searched the data for signs.
Then on a day in 95,the discovery of top blasted worldwide!
The physicists were so happy they almost cried!

In the little quark family,
top was a bit of an anomaly.
Instead of being small and spindly,
top beat the down quark by thirty-five G!

As this all had been going on,
more particles did the small quarks spawn
negative but just the same, the
quarks had antiquarks, who could blame 'em?

When the nights got hard and tough
the two just annihilated in one big PUFF!
Physicists were not satisfied
with simply giving quarks six names
they probed and poked and tried to tame 'em.

They found that to up and charm and top
a two-thirds charge was firmly tied.
Down and strange and of course bottom
measured one-third on the dark side.

Now these charges couldn't be measured
cuz as Gell-Mann said quarks are brothers!
They always go round and round in threes
to keep each other company!

The quarks stick together to form hadrons,
the two types being baryons and mesons.
Baryons made of three positive quarks,
Mesons one positive and one dark.

Quarks have another cool trait,
they come in colors but, please WAIT!
These colors aren't like crayola crayons
the colors are really invisible light bands!

To all the quarks and antiquarks
three colors arc very nicely forked.
Rad Red and Green and Brilliant Blue,
and, of course, the anticolors too!

During strong interactions Quarks have great fun,
exchanging gluons with superb coordination.
When this great, strong gluing dawns,
quarks to each other are nicely hooked on.

Physicists jotted all this info down,
and can smartly identify quarks when found.
Now an important question remains:
Are quarks fundamental or can more be explained?

Poems

HONK IF YOU LOVE ELECTRONS
BY KARA J. WILLIAMS (1997)
ENGLISH MAJOR

is there a universe
inside the universe?
i'm told there is
and my reality denies it.
i believe
my world is what i make it
how i perceive it.
it is what i tell it to be.
but then–
what makes me
to make my world?
where is the beginning of my understanding?
in a way it is comforting
to think there are little pieces of the world
that make me as i make it
colliding
reacting
destroying
creating
me
like me.
the chaos yet
ultimate organization
infinite and finite structures
fundamental composition
(organization)
of particles within atoms
within particles
within life
giving life
from interactions
of the matter that is and the matter that isn't.
energy conservation: amount of energy must remain
constant; cannot be created or destroyed

annihilation: two things come together and only produce
energy or mediators (not particles)
do particles in water get wet?
is something smaller than the whole/a piece of the whole
still the thing itself?
do they cease to be that which they create?
i am partial
to the philosophy
of physics.
can the pattern of masses,
of energy,
be understood?
the substructure that is
the form the shape the framework
of the formshapeframework we know
is still hidden,
lurking in the shadows
suggested
by what is still to be seen.
the postmodern world is physics
but there is no room for science
in the realm of limitless
possibilities meanings interpretations
significance.
where do we locate proof in the quest
for understanding? for self for society
for science
the answer isn't
in this version of the world.
but i believe in quarks
(the word itself deserves faith)
and so perhaps that makes them real
gives the proof
places responsibility with me
for the creation of the universe.
i am created by what i create.

GENESIS OF THE SUB-ATOMIC
BY GREGORY P. LYNCH (1992)
PHILOSOPHY MAJOR

In the beginning, Strong made the Heavens and the Earth.
And Strong saw that it was good, and it was good.
But Strong had only the ability
To rearrange quarks, and not to transform them,
So Strong experimentally discovered the Weak, plus   5
the Gravitational, and the Electromagnetic to complement
them. And here in the void were the Four lonely,
Thus they took the raw mud of the Earth,
these being proton, neutron and electron,
and discovered the Atom, and shaped him according to their 10
own image and likeness and forces.
And the Four saw that this was good, and it was good.
But then the Four were curious, and so
Archangel Rutherford tooketh the Polonium thereof and
shotteth the Alphaic Radiationum   15
through this pudding-like mass called thereof Atom,
and in the year of 1911 discovered the Holy Nucleus. But
This did not satisfy them, for they were but Four,
and the nucleus and the electron were but two.
Thus the numbers had to be more complex of the nucleus,   20
therein. So in the year 1915 the Archangel Chadwick
shotteth more Alphaic Radiationum through a tube
filled within by gas of Nitrogen. When it was
detected, the nuclei of Hydrogen, on the other side,
he knew. And the two Archangels collaborated,   25
and they did shoot more Alphaic Radiationum
toward the sacred Beryllium and the Holy Paraffin, and
duly noticed thereof a plethora of protons. Thus there were
particles flying betweeneth the Sacred Beryllium and the
Holy Paraffin which they could not detect with the help of 30
the Electromagnetic. Thus the empty particle was neutral,
and the Four named it the Neutron, according to its nature.
But the Four were still unsatisfied, for Atom was lonely.
So they took from Atom's side the Neutron, and there was
created Eve, the Neutron. Upon her appearance, Atom   35

and Eve were called over by the Four, who showed
them the tree of Forbidden knowledge.
Upon this tree grew the dooming fruit, the D^+K^-.
Then the Four took nap, so that Atom and Eve
could be naughty without Their sight, in their   40
mercy. And Eve eateth the fruit thereof,
for she, a Neutron, bit a DK.
Thus the Four awoke, and the wrath of the Weak was
the swiftest, and thus the flaming sword, the W-Boson,
changed her neutral udd quarks to positive uud quarks,   45
and thus released an electron and the antineutrino,
of the electron sort. Thus was evil released into the world,
for before had Atom and Eve not known of the antiparticles.
With this new knowledge, they were no longer fit and pure to
exist within the garden, and so they were expelled from it,   50
forthwith, into the madly-rushed world of modern society.
In this world, everyone rusheth about as quickly as possible,
until death when, yea, they were shoved out of this
material plane, back, back into the ethereal world
of Heaven and the Garden. It is said that this   55
material plane is an accelerated
place, and thus the world is called Accelerator.
In the olden times, the inhabitants believed that
Accelerator was flat, and longer in one direction
than in the other. Thus it was a <u>linear</u> Accelerator.   60
But as science grew, the world was round, and so it
was a <u>cyclic</u> Accelerator. This mad world, full of sin and
confusion is a veritable zoo of such inhabitants, the various
tribes of Babylon, all of different types, sizes, charges, spins,
and energies. Hundreds of types were discovered   65
daily, in the dark days of 1940-1960. But through the darkness,
light shone, breaking the clouds apart, by the grace of the Four.
Accelerator's science showeth that such a plethora of particles
could not be the basic building blocks of matter, the geometric
shapes that the patterns of the meson and the hadron and the 70
strange tribes pointed to a symmetry that casteth doubt upon
the Accelerators' false belief of these as fundamental. So the
prophets, Gell-Mann and Zweig in the festival year 1964
put forth for sacrifice the holy tablet of quarks,
which readeth: 75

"There shall be a quark for three types,
the third number being holy, and these three shall be:
up, down, and strange. And so as with each kind
of true quark, there shall be three opposites for each
good quark: the antiup, antidown and antistrange."   80
But the Four, decreeing that the number three was not
holy enough, saw to it that there was a fourth holy
quark type to coincide with the four leptons already
known to the Acceleratorians – the omnipresent electron,
the disappearing muon thrust from the loins of the pious   85
pion, and the invisible guardians of these two,
the electron and muon neutrino. These guardians, invisible
in every respect except for spin, must keep to their
individual appointed tasks, the electron neutrino to the
electron, and the muon neutrino to the muon, as is   90
according to the will of the Four. But the sinful, wild zoo
does not stop there. Two more leptons were discovered, the
enormously fat tau and its guardian particle, the tau neutrino.
So, the Acceleratorians, being smart, hypothesized the
confusing concepts of truth and beauty as two more quarks, 95
building blocks of all there is, save the Four. But the
precocious and prideful Acceleratorians invented color to
separate the particles even further, so that there were Red,
Blue, and Green quarks, and the
antiparticles of a color collected together   100
with much force, and the particles of
same or different color repulsed one another. Thus the
race war beginneth. And the tension was so powerful, that
the hand of the Strong force, the binding force of creation,
the Gluon, was needed to keep different colored   105
quarks together. And so is the world explained by the
Acceleratorians, purely by science and
by no other means, so that the mystery of the world
is taken away with epistemism,
and they all lived happily ever after.
Amen.   111

131

Poems

NEUTRALLY SILLY
BY MEGUMI MATSUKI (2002)
UNDECIDED MAJOR

Poor, poor neutron,
heartedly spinning.
Unhappy with his somber, subatomic self.
He's not like his baryon brother proton—a passionate
positive particle.
And those electrons, so elusively electrically charged, its
negative side is a plus.
Not only is he dull, colorlessly lifelessly dull, but with an
identity crisis to boot.
You see he used to be proud of his fundamental nature.
But then he found out who he really was.
Three quarks.
Three flavorful, colorful quarks.
An up, a down, and a down.
Up, down, down. Up, down, down.
And that's how he felt. Down.
"But I can't even have the blues," he thinks bitterly, blandly
bitterly.
"Quarks get to be blue – or even red or green."
Not even envy can make this fella green.
Where's that little Neutrino when you need him, right,
Neutron?
"Huh, probably getting discovered outside a nuclear reactor.
Well, he should just get used up,
 at Fermilab, or CERN, or Stanford.
He owes me one,
He wouldn't have been discovered if one of my kind hadn't
decayed.
Maybe I should decay…become a proton, electron, and
antineutrino.
But I'm stuck in this nucleus.
Why? Because of the residual strong force… not the
fundamental.
Maybe I should crawl into the beryllium target my folks
came out of.

At least they got to knock some protons out.
Or maybe my antiself has some ideas…
Yeah, I'll talk to him."
Silly particle.
Has living in the nucleus made you dense?
There are plenty of other neutral folks.
Cascade, sigma, pion, kaon—they should knock some sense into you.
Maybe you should talk to neutral delta.
He's up, down, and down too.
Go cheer him up, delta.
Neutron, you completed the atomic picture.
The nucleus would be inadequate without you.
Chadwick loves you.
He discovered you.
Yeah, remember that Chadwick?
And he contains neutrons.
Have you heard of neutron radiography?
That's a useful tool.
And are you sure you want freedom?
You'll last fifteen minutes, tops.
"Oh…"
And, uh, an antineutron could annihilate you.
Think about that.
"Oh…"
Not to add to your crisis,
But do you know about the virtual pion?
Or how about the weak force?
He can change quark types.
Or reactions?
What will you be then?
But for now, be a happy hadron.
A component of the nucleus.
Besides,
Quarks aren't so great,
Are they?
Even they may be made of parts.
Yeah, you'd like to meet a subquark particle, wouldn't you?
Now come on, photon, show him the light.
Help him end his drab dilemma.

FREE VERSE RUMINATION ON QUARKS
BY VANESSA PEPOY (1998)
UNDECIDED MAJOR

<u>Creation</u>
Enigmas.
Three pairs
molding the universe
through their mixing
and re-mixing,
combining capriciously
with their shadow-selves
to form, full and glorious,
cataclysmic stars,
infinitely small particles racing
on light,
humanity.

<u>Chromodynamics</u>
Rouge vert bleu
Trinity of color.
Fundamental.
Organizational.
Principle.
Contained within
a particle,
white light
invisible.

<u>Nuclear Glue</u>
Explicably grouped,
nuclearly restrained by
the strongest of forces.
Outside the precise and
finite diameter,
this mega-force
this goliath
Cannot whimper.
Subatomic irony?

Implications
Loners rocketing,
space-time oblivious
rebelling comprehension.
Undiscovered nomadic tendencies
What can one do solo:
new creation upon entry into
old particle pairings?
Unimaginable freedom,
moving through known dimensions
to… the mind seizes, collapses.
Can we imagine these possibilities
any more than an ant
is aware of a telephone?
Yet quietly taunting us,
knowledge is the sweetest candy.

CLASSIFIEDS/LOST&FOUND/WANTED/
ENTERTAINMENT
BY NOELLE DWYER (2002)
RUSSIAN STUDIES

BULLETIN BOARD:

<u>MISSING!</u> Nan Neutron from Sector A. Missing now 100 seconds. She was last seen at the kickball yard waiting to undergo radioactive beta decay. She has blond hair, weighs 1 unit, and has 1/2 spin and zero electric charge. She is made up of three quarks: two downs and one up. If found please report immediately to the proper authorities.

-

Let's Annihilate each other!
π^- ISO feisty π^+ to share moment of absolute bliss! Please, only positive pions need reply. You, like me, know we've only got a lifetime of 10^{-8} s. So let's get together. Go out with a photon! No use waiting around to decay! I mean if you wait just a split 1/100th of a second too long, it could be too late, you'll have decayed into a positive muon and muon antineutrino. Really, how fun would that be? So if you're looking for a night you'll never forget you've come to the right particle. Mailbox #92.

-

The Kaons, Lambdas, Sigmas and Cascades declare war against crime! The $K\Lambda\Sigma\Xi$ Committee on Crime has organized a meeting, Sunday, March 3, 2002. All particles are welcome but do, please, form orderly lines and stick to your side of the electric field fence during speeches. If you have to decay, please find an usher and he/she will escort you to the proper facilities. Also in response to a growing concern, we expect the number of accidental annihilations to be significantly lower than recent events due to stronger magnets being used to control the crowds of particles.

-

For Sale: Used 1987 L'Accelerator, in Burnt Sienna, 112,398 miles.

Good condition. Great for long road trips when all you want to do when you get to the "motel" is collapse out of energy! Now you can in comfort! Bucket seats, cup holders am/fm stereo…so come on all you pions protons, and neutrons! Sit back. Relax. Have a cup o' Jo. Your kids will love it! Just think the Kaons, Lambdas, Sigmas and Cascades will come into being – blessed event – and you don't want the first thing they see to be patchy old upholstery and the first thing they smell to be french fries and old-car-smell! Do them right and do yourself right - take control of your life and buy this accelerator. Mailbox # 103.

"Existence precedes essence"– Jean Paul Sartre.

ENTERTAINMENT:

NEW FILM SERIES! From producer Aaron Spelling comes a trilogy of sex drugs and rock n' roll. Showing this weekend at the downtown Cineplex is "Not without my Force Carrier" a gripping drama about the electromagnetic force and its mediator, the photon. Coming Summer 2003: "All About My Gluons," the touching story of the 8 gluons and how they mediate the Strong Force. "My Life as a W or Z Boson," a mock documentary about the inner workings of the force carriers for the weak force. Watch for fabulous special effects especially during the scenes of quark transformations.

-Also, this year at the ever popular Cannes Film Festival director Cameron Crowe will speak about his new film, "Almost Famous," the secret life of the Higgs Boson.

-

P(article)TV this week:

Sunday: Karma-To Be or Not to See? Jane Pauly investigates the concept of Karma and whether it applies to any subatomic particles. Plus! A live interview with a positive Kaon right before decay and its products right after the decay. This is a topic no particle should miss!

Monday: E! Celebrity Profile talks with the elusive, very hard to catch Charm Quark. Come, join Jules Asner in getting the dish on this particle, who is 1.5 times as massive as the proton with a charge of +2/3. E! Extra! A live radiocast of this interview is available on the GeV and TeV scale. Call in and ask her anything and everything, like, is there competition between the quarks? Does everyone get along?

-

Tuesday: Lifetime TV for Women brings you "Never Cry Nucleon: The Susan Lucci Story." Ever wonder why it took Susan Lucci 12 nominations for best actress in a daytime soap for her to finally win? Get the inside track on her subatomic particles. What makes Susan Lucci tick? Is she really a nucleon? Watch and find out what it was like to live and work in the nucleus of NBC's hottest soap.

-

Wednesday:
All new Survivor: Lepton Collider. Join contenders, electron, positron, muon and antimuon as they battle for existence. Go behind the scenes of the new Lepton Collider and see what really happens when leptons stop being nice and start getting real.

GLOSSARY

Annihilation: When a matter/antimatter pair of particles meets and turns into energy. For annihilation to occur, it must be an exact matter/antimatter pair. An electron can annihilate with a positron and a proton can annihilate an antiproton. A positron and antiproton cannot annihilate each other. The amount of energy produced by the annihilation is equal to the sum of the masses of the particles involved.

Antiparticle: An antiparticle has the opposite properties of its particle when there is an opposite (like charge and strangeness, for example), and the same value for properties that do not have possible opposites (like mass). Every known particle has an antiparticle.

Baryon: A hadron with half-integer spin. All baryons are composed of three quarks. The most common baryons are the proton and the neutron.

Beta decay: When a neutron decays into a proton, an electron, and an antineutrino. The underlying process is a down quark changing into an up quark, an electron, and an antineutrino. The weak interaction is responsible for beta decay.

Cascade: A strange baryon. The cascade particle comes in two types. One type is negatively charged and one is neutral. Each cascade particle contains two strange quarks.

Collider: An accelerator in which two beams of particles circulate in opposite directions and collide head-on. Currently colliders are capable of producing collisions of particles with the highest energies. The top quark was discovered at t he collider at Fermilab, the Tevatron.

Conservation: A conserved quantity is one that has the same value before and after a process. Examples of quantities that are conserved in various types of interactions are baryon number, charge, energy, lepton number, momentum, and strangeness.

Decay: The process of one particle becoming two or more particles. Most particles are not stable and therefore they decay. For example a pion decays into a muon and two neutrinos.

Detector: Any device that can sense the presence of a particle and give information about one or more of its properties. Detectors are usually used to measure speed, mass, charge and energy. They are typically connected to complicated electronics and the information gathered is passed on to very fast computers for further analysis.

Electromagnetic force: Force that acts between all charged objects. It can be attractive or repulsive. The electromagnetic force is infinite in range and is mediated by the photon. The farther away two charged objects are, the weaker the electromagnetic force between them.

Electron: A fundamental particle with negative electric charge. It is one of the three constituents of the atom. The electron is a stable particle and therefore does not decay.

Force: That which governs the interaction between particles. There are four known fundamental forces: electromagnetic, gravitational, strong, and weak.

Force carrier: The particle exchanged during an interaction. Force carriers are also called mediators.

Generation: Two leptons and two quarks together form a generation. The electron, its neutrino, and the up and down quarks form the first generation. The muon, its neutrino, and the charm and strange quarks form the second generation. The tau, its neutrino, and the top and bottom quarks form the third generation.

Gluon: The mediator of the strong force. There is strong experimental evidence for the existence of gluons inside of particles like the proton. Free gluons have not yet been observed although currently there are experiments looking for "glueballs".

Graviton: The mediator of the gravitational force. The graviton has never been observed in an experiment but in order for theories to be complete they should exist.

Gravitational force: The force that acts between all objects with mass. It is always attractive. The gravitational force is the binding force of the universe. It is a very important force to us. It keeps the moon revolving around the earth and the earth revolving around the sun. It is a force that gets smaller as the distance between masses decreases.

Hadron: Any particle that experiences the strong force. Hadrons are further composed of two groups, the baryons and the mesons.

Kaon: A strange meson with about half the proton mass. Kaons can be positive, neutral or negative and they are unstable particles. They live for an extremely short time before decaying into other particles.

Kinetic energy: Energy of motion. Only objects that are moving have kinetic energy. As the speed of a particle increases, it's kinetic energy increases.

Lambda: A strange baryon. The lambda is neutral and contains one strange quark. Lambdas are not stable and decay typically into protons or neutrons .

Lepton: Considered to be a fundamental particle. There are six known leptons: the electron, the muon, the tau, and three neutrinos. They do not experience the strong force.

Lifetime: The average time that an unstable particle (or atom or nucleus) lives before decaying into other particles (or atoms or nuclei).

Linear accelerator: A machine that accelerates charged particles in a straight path. Linear accelerators are the simplest to build and operate but they must be very, very long to accelerate particles to high energies.

Meson: A hadron with integer spin. Mesons are always composed of a quark and an antiquark. They are hadrons, which means they are affected by the strong force. Pions and kaons are the most commonly produced mesons.

Muon: A fundamental lepton with a mass of about 200 times the electron mass. Muons are negatively charged and antimuons are positively charged. Muons are capable of passing through a lot of material before they interact or decay.

Neutrino: A fundamental lepton that has no electric charge and little or no mass. There are three kinds of neutrinos: electron neutrino, muon neutrino, and tau neutrino. Each neutrino has a corresponding antineutrino.

Neutron: A constituent of the nucleus. It has no electric charge and is made of three quarks: two downs and one up. The neutron is generally stable when it is inside of a nucleus. A free neutron will decay with a lifetime of about 15 minutes.

Nucleon: The collective name for protons and neutrons.

Nucleus: The densest part of an atom, it contains protons and neutrons.

Pair production: The opposite of annihilation, when electromagnetic energy becomes a pair of particles. In order for pair production to occur there must be enough energy. In order for a proton and antiproton production to occur, the electromagnetic energy must be at least equal to twice the mass of the proton.

Photon: The carrier of the electromagnetic force. Photons are also called gamma rays or gamma radiation.

Pion: A meson with a mass of 1/7 the proton. Pions can be positive, negative or neutral and they are unstable. Pions contain a quark and an antiquark.

Positron: The antiparticle of the electron. Positrons were discovered in the 1930's and are not only interesting in particle physics. They are used in many practical ways in medicine.

Proton: A constituent of the nucleus. It has positive electric charge and is made of three quarks: two ups and one down. The proton is a stable particle.

Quark: Considered a fundamental particle according to the standard model. There are six flavors of quarks: up, down, strange, charm, bottom, and top. They are distinguished from each other by their charges and masses. Up, charm and top have positive charge and down, strange and bottom have negative charges. The lightest ones are up and down and the top is the heaviest .

Radiation: That which is emitted from an atom, nucleus, or particle. Alpha radiation is the emission of a helium nucleus, beta radiation is the emission of an electron (and antineutrino), and gamma radiation is high-energy photon emission.

Reaction: Two particles interacting to produce one or more particles.

Scintillator: A material that emits light when struck by a charged particle. Scintillation counters are used to detect charged particles.

Sigma: A strange baryon that is slightly more massive than the proton. The sigma can be positive, negative or neutral and each kind contains one strange quark.

Spin: An intrinsic property that a particle may possess. Leptons and quarks, the fundamental particles, have 1/2 unit of spin. Mesons have integer spins (0,1,2...) and baryons have half-integer spins (1/2, 3/2, 5/2, ...).

Standard Model: A model of six quarks and six leptons as fundamental entities. Currently commonly accepted although there are things that the Standard Model does not explain.

Strong force: The force that acts between all nucleons. It is attractive for all combinations of protons and neutrons. Quarks feel the strong force, but leptons do not.

Tau: A fundamental lepton with a mass of about 3,600 times the electron mass. The tau particle has a negative charge and the antitau has a positive charge.

W mediators: The charged carriers of the weak force. The W's can be positive or negative and they are almost 100 times as massive as a proton.

Weak force: The force that can change one quark type into another. It is the only force affecting neutrinos.

Z mediator: The neutral carrier of the weak force. It is almost 100 times as massive as a proton.

Suggestions for Further Reading

Schwarz, Cindy. *A Tour of the Subatomic Zoo – A Guide to Particle Physics*, AIP Press, 1997.

Close, F. *The Cosmic Onion*, American Institute of Physics, New York, 1986.

Close, F., M. Marten and C. Sutton. *The Particle Explosion*, Oxford University Press, Oxford, 1987.

Kane, Gordon. *The Particle Garden: Our Universe as Understood by Particle Physicists*, Addison Wesley, (1995),

Web sites

Cindy Schwarz's home page
http://faculty.vassar.edu/schwarz/

Great web site http://particleadventure.org

To order additional books go to the web site
www.smallworldbooks.net